Falling for the Quarterback

A Novella

Clearview Falls University
Book 4

S.E. Rose

Sierra Hill

Prologue

Clearview Ski Resort - March
Charlotte

"So how about that drink?"

The man I just met and who practically saved my life on the ski slope winks and motions toward the lobby of the ski resort. "I know a better place than that one." He offers me a large hand expectantly.

With a furtive glance around the quiet lodge area, I cautiously accept it, feeling the warmth of his palm immediately spread through the length of my arm. Then I wonder if it's wise to trust a man I just met.

However, he did just save me. That counts for something, right? Had it not been for his quick actions, the ski patrol would've been peeling my mangled limbs from that tree I nearly crashed into earlier.

One minute I'm on my feet and the next, I'm being tugged into his side, held steady and upright against his body. This man has some amazing strength and reaction time. With a palm to the curve of my lower back, he guides me past the posh lobby bar and outside the front doors of the lodge.

"Where are we going?" There's a slight rise at the end of my question and I wonder if I should say yes.

"You'll see. It's just down the back."

The snow crunches underneath our snow boots as we walk along a stone path toward the back of the lodge, where the smell of an outdoor fire rises through the crisp air. He leads me toward a small shack that looks like something out of a *Hobbit* movie, with a thatched roof covered in snow. I breathe out a slight sigh of relief that he didn't drag me into the woods like my imagination suggested. As we enter, I get a glimpse of the low-lit room, with its all-alpine woods and dark corners and a giant stone hearth that has a warm fire burning in it.

It makes for a cozy and romantic hideaway, and I instantly feel the effects as he locates us two seats at a small table near the back of the bar.

He pulls out the chair for me and I take a seat, covering the back of it with my ski jacket. He raises a finger to grab the attention of the bartender, a beast of a man who could easily pass for a lumberjack. Jake, his name tag says, rounds the corner of the bar and he steps up to our table.

"Haven't seen you in a while, Hendy," Jake says, giving a bro handshake to the man I'm with. "What can I get you two?"

"What would you like?" my potential bad decision asks as he turns toward me with a smile that could melt glaciers.

My thoughts are still wrapped around the idea that this man—*Hendy, as I've now learned*—is a known entity to the bartender, which eases my worries exponentially. At the very least, if I suddenly disappear, Jake could tell the authorities I was last seen with Hendy.

"A chardonnay," I croak dryly, tacking on a small smile of my own. While a shot of some whiskey would do better in calming my nerves, hard liquor would also make my bad decisions increase tenfold.

I think back to what my best friend Poppy suggested earlier this afternoon during our phone call.

"Have some fun. Maybe you could even meet a handsome cowboy or hot ski instructor on the slopes."

My gaze refocuses on Hendy, as the heat of his eyes on me has me radiating from the inside out.

"Good choice. I'll have a Clase Azul Reposado on the rocks," he says. The bartender nods and lumbers off to make our drinks. It gives me a chance to ask a follow up question to what I've learned so far.

"Sounds like you're a regular here...*Hendy?* Is that your name?"

He chuckles, leaning casually back in his seat with the tilt of his head. "Yep. That's what they call me."

"I'm Lottie," I state matter-of-factly, choosing to use my childhood nickname for some reason. It feels less restrictive than my full name. And since I'm stepping way out of my normal comfort zone tonight, why not try it on for size?

Hendy hand reaches across the table looking for mine. I place my hand in his and he leans over and kisses my knuckles. A shiver runs up my arm and down my spine.

"It's a pleasure to meet you, lovely Lottie."

"Such a gentleman," I tease with a playful laugh, trying to remember any of the rules of flirting. It's been so long.

His eyebrows shoot up toward the fringe of his dark, messy hair. "Hmm...I can be when I want to."

Jake returns with the drinks and sets them down in front of us, departing with a very visible wink at Hendy.

"To a memorable evening with a beautiful woman." He hoists his glass off the table and I do the same.

I blush—because when was the last time someone called me beautiful?—then shake my head and we tap our glasses together. Sipping our drinks, we stare at each other over the rims of our glasses, and a million questions pop in my head.

"Well, why don't you tell me something about yourself, Hendy?" I say in an effort to sound casual. "All I know at this point is you save reckless skiers out on the slopes and know the bartender. Which tells me you come here a lot."

His lips quirk up to the side and the brights of his eyes shine with mystique. He raises a hand, bringing the glass to his lips, and his shirt's fabric clings tight to his bicep. Damn, this man has incredible definition. I felt it earlier when his arms were tightened around my body as he held me upright, saving me from danger. My eyes automatically scan over his face and down his chest where the skin-tight shirt pulls over the grooves of his abdominals.

He cocks his head to one side and regards me quietly. "I come up as often as I can. And, if you must know, I once won a chess competition."

My eyes widen. "Really? You play chess?"

He nods. "As a kid, my dad taught me. It wasn't that hard to learn," he admits with a sheepish grin. "What about you? You're obviously not from around here. Where are you from?"

I set my wine down and let my mind flip through my childhood memories but answer his first question. "I'm here on holiday from the East Coast."

Hendy narrows his eyes at me, disbelieving my statement. I chuckle. "Fine, I've been living on the East Coast.

I'm originally from the UK. And when I was around six or seven, I found a missing dog and received a monetary reward for his return."

"Wow. It seems I'm in the presence of a real Sherlock Holmes," he teases, a slow grin parting at his mouth.

That smile of his is deadly.

He casually sets down his drink and his index finger brushes against mine. The touch—albeit quick—makes my breath hitch. As if waiting to see how I respond, he does it again, this time purposefully rubbing his finger along mine.

An electric current runs through my body, surging over my skin, racing in my bloodstream as desire explodes between my legs. Underneath my sweater, my nipples harden, and I stare at his face. His grin turns into a wicked smile that etches across his lips.

It's that smile that is my undoing. He's going to be my one-night stand.

Tonight. Now.

I reach for my drink and drain it, suddenly needing a little liquid courage. He mirrors me and sets down his empty glass.

We both speak at the same time.

"Would you like another?"

"Let's get out of here," I state boldly, not even recognizing my own voice. "Unless...I'm being presumptuous."

Oh shit. Now I feel like a fool. What if he's married? Has a girlfriend? Isn't interested?

I want to backpedal and erase what I just said.

But from the heated look in his eyes, he's all in.

He pulls out some money from his pocket, tosses it on the table and then stands. Holding out his hand to me, I take it, along with the acceptance of my decision that this is going to happen.

"Your place or mine?" he asks, standing behind me as he helps me into my coat. His voice is deep and low, and the warmth of his breath fans over my neck. It startles me how powerful it is.

He must take this as anxiety, because he whispers in my ear.

"I'm not a serial killer, if that's what you're worried about. In fact, you can leave your name and number with Jake if it makes you feel better. I've also never been arrested," he says with a smirk.

He's one cocky bastard, but secretly it thrills me. He's working to establish trust and make me feel more confident with him.

"Just because you haven't been arrested could just mean you haven't been caught yet," I point out, feeling sassy and buoyant with excitement now.

A deep laugh reverberates from his chest and his hand grasps my hand in his as we leave the bar. I suck in a breath. This man is doing things to me with just the barest of touches and the sound of his voice has my core clenching deliciously in ways it hasn't in years.

"Touché."

I contemplate his question about where we should go. If I'm going to make a bad decision tonight, at least I should have the home-court advantage.

"Let's go to mine. You can follow me. I'm just a mile up the road." I say as he leads us out to the parking lot, his hand returning to the small of my back.

The minute we get to the house and we've removed our outerwear, the electricity crackles and vibrates around us. I secretly want to pat myself on the back for being brave enough to pick up this hot as hell man. He's young, gorgeous, and has biceps that look like I could hang from them.

Fuck me.

"I plan to," he whispers in a sexy, throaty voice as he steps into my body, running his nose along my neck, and then plants his lips there.

Oh shit. I said that out loud.

I let out a sharp gasp when he picks me up to carry me down the hallway, and I wrap my legs around his waist.

"Just show me the way."

I point him toward the bedroom and as he sets me down on the edge of the bed, I raise my palm to his chest.

"Just to be clear, this is only for one night. Not the weekend," I state, my body weeping with need as he stands before me and whips his shirt off his torso.

His hair is messy and his glacier-blue eyes have turned into a dark winter storm.

"I can work with that."

It's a good thing I laid down that rule because he's just the type of man I could fall for too easily.

I have too much ahead of me to want anything more than a one fun and sex-filled night with Hendy.

Chapter One

C harlotte – Earlier that Day

"Well? How did it go? Should I start calling you *Professor* from here on out?"

I chuckle at my best friend's question. It's just like Poppy to put the proverbial cart before the horse. She's always been on my side since we met in the first year of uni as Freshers and one of my biggest advocates. Especially during the challenging times in my life over the past five years.

I, on the other hand, am a bit more reluctant to jump on that moving train until I've received an official offer and the new position is confirmed.

"I think I did well in the panel interview," I offer, recalling the six faces that stared at me across the university conference room table. "They seemed impressed with some of my research papers and asked a lot about my dissertation."

"Of course they did! You're bloody brilliant and they'd be lucky to have your beauty and brains at their Hicksville university."

I make a scolding noise into the speaker phone, gathering up my toiletries from the hotel bathroom and stuffing them in my suitcase. "It's small, by comparison, yes. But Clearview Falls has a wonderful rich history as one of the top schools in the West."

"Pish...but it's not Cambridge," she argues, a whine in her sultry British voice.

I snort. "Thank God for that. I'm very glad to be in the US and not back home."

There's a pause and I can hear her light a cigarette on the other end of the line. It's late back in the UK, and I know she's just returned home from a date.

A pang of homesickness flits through my belly at the memories we shared all those years ago during uni and our subsequent absence when I moved to the East Coast for my PhD program.

"Did they give you a definitive answer on when they'd make their decision and when you'd hear back?"

"Not soon enough. The dean said they'll be finishing up their interviews this week and then making decisions the following. But you know how long these things take. It could be months."

"What does that mean for you?" she asks, exhaling a breath over the line. "Will you stay there in the mountains until a decision is made? You have nothing to rush back to Boston for, after all."

Don't I know it. There is nothing and no one keeping me there. In fact, I have no plans if I don't get this role as an assistant professor on a tenure-track. No other prospects at the moment. And I certainly don't want to return to Cambridge with my pride in my hands and have to live with my father.

"Yes, I think I'm going to take Ana up on her offer and check out her mountain chalet for the weekend."

Poppy hoots in excitement. "That's exactly what you need! Time to let your hair down a bit and relax. You deserve it. And maybe you could even meet a handsome cowboy or hot ski instructor on the slopes."

"Poppy," I admonish, but fight the smile that cracks across my lips. "Why must everything always boil down to meeting men?"

Poppy really is a great friend. Even though we're an ocean apart, she's always there for me. But we also have differing viewpoints on relationships. She sees them all as a waste of time and I still have an old-fashioned belief that there's someone out there for me and someday—hopefully soon—I'll meet him.

"*Why?*" she drawls out loudly. "Because, my darling dearest, a vibrator alone just doesn't cut it."

We talk for another five minutes and then end the call with me promising to let her know as soon as I hear anything from Dean Becker. Then I text both my parents to let them know how my interviews went and set the phone to *Do Not Disturb* as I finish packing my bags. I'll save their questions for later.

Checking around the room one last time to ensure I haven't left anything behind, I drag my suitcase to the rental car and throw it in the boot. Then I type in the address to my cousin Ana's mountain retreat and set a course for the trip.

In less than forty-five minutes, I'm pulling up to a giant

ski chalet home in the mountain forest with a gorgeous wood and river rock exterior that screams, 'Rich people own me.'

I suppose I shouldn't judge, considering my childhood. It's given me the opportunity to attend the best universities in the UK and the US and now allows me to enjoy some much-needed downtime after the hellishly exhausting year I've just endured. Shaking my head clear of those thoughts, I pull up to the large three-car garage drive and park my rental before stepping out into the chilly air.

The crisp, fresh scent of snow and pine trees alights my senses, the air so clean and the sky so clear that I already feel rejuvenated.

The air here in the mountains is so vastly different from the cities I've called home on the East Coast these past few years. And far from the English countryside where I grew up.

Grabbing my bags, I head to the front door of Ana's home. When she heard from my mom that I would be here for my interview, she immediately called to offer me the retreat. Ana is British but married a brilliant American businessman twenty-some years ago and they now live their best life, as evidenced by the ginormous home I walk into after entering the code she'd given me to disarm the alarm.

I'd originally objected to the idea of staying the weekend because I didn't have any ski apparel or equipment with me in Boston. But that problem was quickly remedied when Ana said, "I have more than plenty for you to use."

Boy, she wasn't kidding. When I open the door to the oversized wardrobe, I'm confronted with dozens of various ski pants and jackets to choose from. Yet as I stare into the cavernous closet, a tinge of loneliness spreads through my heart. It feels as vast as this space in front of me. But instead of full, mine is just plain empty.

Maybe Poppy was right. I don't need a man or a relationship, but I do need someone to talk with and have fun with. A dog might work, but maybe finding a hot stranger to hook up with will help rebuild my self-confidence and help me move on from my past.

That's what this is about, right? I need sex. Not a relationship, just hot, exciting *sex*.

I grab one of Ana's evening outfits for later and peruse the insanely opulent bathroom, then decide to take an *everything* shower.

Everything is going to be waxed, shaved, buffed, and beautified before I head to the bar at the nearby ski resort down the road. From there, I'll strike up a conversation with a stranger and set a course for the rest of the evening.

First things first, though. Using Ana's super expensive body and hair products, I take a luxuriating shower and as I towel dry off, I decide I'd like to check out the slopes today and go for one run down the mountain before I head to the restaurant and bar. I've always loved skiing into the dusky hours and haven't done it in forever.

Choosing a fashionable ski outfit with bright yellow and orange patterns, I grab a pair of boots and skis and toss them into my car. The ski resort is a mile back down the road and I passed it on my way here, so the drive is only five minutes, depending on the slippery conditions.

The resort lobby is lavish and bougie, with gorgeous western red cedar and pine varieties of timber that make up the walls and trim. As I make my way to the ski desk, I pass a stone fireplace with a massive hearth and masonry reaching the ceiling, a roaring fire blazing inside.

I purchase my tickets for the weekend and hop on the

ski lift just outside and to the left of the parking lot. The view is spectacular as I arrive at the top of the black diamond path. Staring down the steep ski slope, regret and dread immediately take hold. Maybe my decision to take the most daring run isn't such a great idea after all.

I take deep breaths, getting a tight grip on my poles in my gloved hands, and find my courage. I haven't skied in years. What was I thinking? I glance over at the ski lift and then back down at the trail.

Fuck it. I can do this.

I adjust my goggles over my nose and push off with the toe of my right ski to start a zigzag motion down the mountain. The late afternoon sun's rays shine bright into my eyes through the ski goggles and the cold wind whips against the material of my jacket as I whiz toward the bottom of the run. Feeling warm and more daring now, I pick up speed and fly through the powdery snow toward the bottom of the slope. My limbs are loose and my confidence soars as muscle memory takes over.

I've never felt better or more alive. It's exactly the boost I needed today.

After living with a man like my father constantly controlled my life, the freedom of doing exactly what I want, when I want, is an amazing feeling.

Soon I'm nearly halfway down the slope when I encounter an icy snowbank. The tips of my skis tangle together and my torso tips forward from the momentum as I begin to lose my balance.

"Oh, shit!" I cry out in a panicky screech, my eyes catching on the immovable tree coming up fast in front of me.

And then out of nowhere comes a response.

"I got you."

Suddenly, there are another pair of skis next to me and two strong hands cinching around my waist to stabilize my balance and keep me upright. We both turn to face one another, our eyes wide as I realize we've come to an abrupt stop just before slamming into the massive fir tree mere inches from our bodies.

"Bloody hell!" I whisper in awe, blinking rapidly as my body shakes from both the adrenaline rush and utter relief that I'm still alive and unmaimed.

The man laughs and he slowly releases his hold on me, removing his goggles from his face. Then he quirks a crooked smile. "You can say that again. Although I probably would've said fucking hell."

My expression likely appears baffled as I stare at him, mystified by how he materialized out of thin air. Is he real or my guardian angel?

I inhale, hoping to regain my composure, but a whiff of his woodsy scent has me nearly swooning. The masculinity of the scent and his strong pair of arms, and perhaps a mixture of pheromones has my lady parts activating for the first time in...well, months. Or has it been over a year?

"Thank you," I manage to croak out once I've steadied myself on my skies, shoving my poles securely into the snow. "I'm not sure where you came from, but it was fortuitous timing."

His eyebrows shoot up and disappear under his hat. "Whoa, fancy words in a British accent. You might just melt the snow with all that hotness if you're not careful."

He gives me a slow, easy smile, and it confounds me. Is this man flirting with me? First he saves me and then he teases me in a sexy, cocky way?

Did I hit my head on that tree and not know it?

The man clears his throat when I don't respond.

"Anyway, it might be a good idea if I follow you down. Is that okay with you?" he offers, motioning with a pole back toward the trail.

"Oh, yes, thank you. I'd appreciate that." The words come out in a breathless rush. His smile widens and he waggles his brows before lowering his goggles.

The man follows closely behind and in a matter of minutes, we're down the mountain and back at the resort.

As I slide to a stop and pause near the path that leads toward the parking lot, he maneuvers up next to me, shoving his poles into the snow and sliding his goggles once more to the top of his head. When I do the same and get my first good look at him, I nearly gasp. Now that I see him without the haze of a near death experience, I'm at a loss for words.

This man is definitely a decade younger than me and also one of the most attractive men I've ever laid eyes on. His face is covered in a well-trimmed beard of blondish-brown hair and his glacial blue eyes seem to sparkle against the reflected light from the snow. He's taller than I am by a good six inches and his broad shoulders under the ski jacket look very strong, his frame blocking my view of everything behind him.

He has the build of an athlete or someone who takes fastidious care of their body. It could be from skiing, but I would guess some other type of sport. It's not his body that has me doing something I've never done before. It's the intensity of his blue gaze.

I flirt.

"I feel like I should thank you for your assistance," I say coyly with the bite of my lip.

Maybe this man could be my one-night stand? The thought fills my belly with a fluttering sensation.

He could very well be a serial killer for all I know, but as long as he fucks me before he kills me, it's worth the risk.

"Oh, yeah?" he replies, popping his skis off as I do the same and holding them in one gloved hand.

"I mean, a *proper* thank you," I add, batting my eyelashes as seductively as I can.

"Proper, eh?" he asks in a teasing voice, trying to mimic a British accent and failing spectacularly. It's rather cute.

"Care to join me for a drink?" I motion toward the ski lodge behind us; there must be multiple bars in a place this size.

It's completely out of character for me. I've never been one to invite a man for a drink. Especially a man I don't know. But in this case, I'm throwing all caution to the wind and going for it because he's a very attractive man.

Without taking even a second to pause and consider my invitation, the man replies.

"Sure, I've got no other plans. I'd love to."

Chapter Two

J oel - September

"Dude, look who's back on campus!"

"It's Hendy! Bro, good to see you."

"Get your ass over here, Hendy! How the fuck you been, man?"

I stride into the student center, a CFU ball cap pulled low over my eyes, hoping to remain unnoticed by the other students congregating in the café.

No such luck.

Even incognito, I'm a recognizable feature on campus and have many fans and acquaintances from my former ball-playing days. *Former.* As in, no longer their QB One.

The thought is depressing as fuck. I knew this transition would be tough getting through the final year in my graduate program, but it's proving more difficult than I expected.

In the past when I walked into a room and was recognized as a local legend, it boosted my ego to receive all the attention as the star quarterback for the CFU Bears. I was like a king on campus and treated like one.

But now? Not this year. This year, I'm just a regular Joe Schmoe grad student.

Nothing special about me, aside from my championship titles and an elite position in the school's football Hall of Fame history.

I shake off the depressing thoughts that infiltrate my brain and plaster on a smile, aiming it at the group of lowerclassman all hanging out in the middle of the student lounge. Each one either slaps me on my back, gives me a fist bump, or high-fives me.

The two girls, one blonde and the other a redhead, smile sweetly and bat their eyelashes at me, giggling coyly and whispering to each other as I approach. In the past, their interest in me boosted my ego and fed my self-importance. Now it feels a little fake and disingenuous because I'm not that guy anymore. Or at least, I want to be. I'm done with football and all the drama.

If this is how my little sister, Journey, chooses to act around athletes on campus this year as an incoming freshman, I'm going to have to lock her away in her dorm for the entire school year. I'm already worried about her fitting in and adjusting to campus life, even though my friends Grace, Lucy, and Kelsie have all assured me they'll take her under their wings.

"Hey guys, how was your summer?" My question is directed toward the two senior frat guys, Layton and Sean, who I know from previous years' parties at the Kappa Sigma Pi frat house. They are both total douches and probably haven't matured much since last year.

The taller of the two, Sean, jumps to his feet from his spot on top of the café table and pulls out his phone. Swiping the screen open, he taps it once and shoves it in front of my face.

"Check this out, bro. We went hiking and waterskiing in Tahoe in July and then partied our asses off in Vegas. It was fucking lit, man!"

I'm not the least bit interested in his photos but smile and nod regardless, making a mental note to keep my sister as far away from these asshats as possible.

Layton joins in, laughing darkly. "Fuck, bro, we got so wasted one night at Club Chic, I think I passed out between some topless chick's tits."

"Hmm." It's all I can think of to say because it only confirms these two are idiot man-children who only think with their dicks and have no purpose in life other than to party and get laid.

You were the same in the past.

The two start reminiscing with each other and it gives me the opportunity I need to get the hell out of here.

"Good catching up, guys," I say, looking for my exit just as my name is being called by a feminine voice across the room.

Thank God. Saved by Grace. *Literally.*

Grace and Lucy are over in line at the coffee bar, waiting for their drinks. I wave in their direction.

"See ya. I gotta meet my friends and get to class."

I turn to go when the blonde girl grabs hold of my forearm, her delicate grip on my skin foreign and all wrong. I glance down at it and then at her as she smiles up at me with plump lips.

"Mind if I walk with you, Hendy? I'd love to hear what you did all summer."

As gently as I can so as not to be disrespectful, I pry her pink fingernails from my arm and drop it to her side.

"Sorry, uh..." I'm trying to recall if she gave me her name or not.

She pouts. "You don't remember me? It's Maisy."

Shit. Nope. Don't remember her at all.

"Maisy. I'm sorry, but I really gotta go. But I'll see you around, 'kay?"

This somehow cheers her up, her eyes dancing with excitement. "Will you be at the first home game this weekend and the Kappa party after?"

I almost flinch. Not necessarily because of her question, but that the connotation is so different than it used to be for me. Had this been last year, of course I would have gone to the post-game party. I was the goddamn quarterback and star of the team. I would have played the game and gone to whatever house party was being thrown in our team's honor, where I would've gotten drunk and probably laid.

This year, however, none of my friends will be playing —except Hayes McIntyre, who was new last year. He's still the kicker on the team and is Kelsie's boyfriend.

If EJ and Killian plan to visit this weekend, then I'll definitely go to the game, but not the frat party. We'll just be low-key chilling at the off-campus house I used to share with them.

I shrug noncommittally. "I don't know. We'll see. Depends on how much studying I have to do this weekend."

Maisy pouts again, this time with an added flare of downcast eyes and a syrupy sweet voice. "That sounds so boring. Wouldn't you rather come with me and have some fun?"

Fun. I remember the last time I truly had fun. And I haven't been able to get her out of my head for months.

Jesus, I'm almost getting a boner thinking about her now.

To avoid any embarrassing and unwanted attention, I raise my eyebrows skyward at Maisy, brushing a hand over my chin where my short-clipped beard would be if I hadn't shaved it off last weekend.

"Nobody ever said a graduate program was fun. I'll see ya round, Maisy."

Without any further awkwardness, I turn on my heels and beeline it over to join the girls. Gracie waggles her eyebrows as I approach.

"Always on the prowl, aren't you, Hendy?"

I roll my eyes, giving a half-glance over my shoulder to ensure Maisy has retreated from earshot.

"That wasn't on me this time. Shocker, I know."

Lucy chuckles and hands me a drip coffee and two creamers. She turns to Grace next to her. "Oh, Gracie. Our boy is finally growing up!"

I accept the coffee in one hand and nudge her with my shoulder against hers. "Shut it, you brat, or I'll tell EJ you're flirting with the barista dude."

Lucy scoffs and flicks a gaze over at Damon, the guy behind the espresso maker who happens to glance up and smiles congenially.

"You wouldn't," she argues. "Plus, Emmett wouldn't believe you. He knows I can't flirt."

I laugh. "That's true. You tried with me and failed miserably!"

She moves to swat my arm but I dodge away, narrowly missing a tall woman with a severe reddish-blonde bun tied neatly at her nape who walks past us with her head in her phone on our way to the door. Something about her posture and the way she stands pushes at the recesses of my mind, but Grace's question steals my attention back.

"What's your first class today? Which building?" Grace asks as I open the door and allow them to walk out in front of me. I blink and shield my eyes from the bright glare of the sunshine that has just risen over the mountain tops.

"It's over in Cameron Hall. Digital Marketing Case Studies of European Countries."

Neither seems too impressed by the title, and truthfully, neither was I when I first enrolled.

I still have no idea what I want to do with my life. Since I doubled up on graduate level courses as a senior last year, I now only have a year of coursework left. But there are still moments when I'm really bummed I didn't at least attempt to go out for the NFL draft, but I knew it was a longshot. While I was a great D2 quarterback, my standing and abilities likely wouldn't have made the cut, and I didn't want to be rejected in that way.

Say what you will about my cocky attitude, I'm actually quite thin-skinned. I take rejection hard.

"Sounds cool. Do you know the professor from your undergrad classes?"

I shake my head. "Nah. I think they may be new to the school this year. Someone named C. Butler. Don't know anything about them. Their bio and picture wasn't even on the university website yet when I checked last week. Guess I'm about to find out."

The girls take their turns throwing their arms around me to say goodbye and I hug them back.

"Well, I hope it's a fun class!" Lucy chirps. "See you at home later."

And with that, I head off to Cameron Hall.

Chapter Three

C harlotte

Nerves have settled in my belly, jostling the three bites of toast I ate earlier for breakfast, as I decide on my first day of class attire. Searching my wardrobe, I begin rifling through all my clothing options, which honestly feel too similar to Queen Elizabeth's matronly attire. Old and outdated.

I grouse at my decision not to go shopping before I started my position. Although, to be fair, I didn't have a lot of time because I only had three weeks to move once they made me the offer.

Finally narrowing it down, I select button-down cream top and a pair of high-waisted black pleated trousers with a large black belt. Looking in the full-length mirror, I realize the black bra I'm wearing can clearly be seen through the top's material, so I exchange it for a white lace one, then fiddle with the buttons on the blouse. I don't want to look too conservative, so I unbutton the top two pearl buttons and check to make sure neither my cleavage nor my bra can be seen.

Satisfied I look the part, I wrap my long strawberry-blonde hair low against my nape and tie it into a tight bun to keep it from falling into my face. Then I touch up my makeup and add some mascara before I leave the small off-campus bungalow the university has rented me for the academic year.

Although my interview was back in March—during my infamous one-night-stand with Hendy—the university took its sweet time in finally offering me a tenure-track position in the business school just three weeks ago. My teaching and classes are mainly focused on digital marketing and the European markets, and I'll have three graduate program classes this semester while I also begin my research paper on global marketing management.

There were only a few weeks to get everything in order back in Boston, then drive my belongings out west and get situated in Clearview Falls. I've barely had time to acclimate myself to campus since I arrived in town.

The beauty of living so close to this gorgeous university is I can walk the five blocks along tree-lined streets. Sure, Boston had all the seasons, but it didn't have the lush landscape of trees and mountainous background where fall is just beginning to begin show through the change of colors.

As I make it to the quad on campus, I look around in awe at how vastly my life has changed this past year. Starting today, all my hopes and dreams and everything I've worked for all these years have come to fruition.

God, I hope I do well. I *need* this job. I've given everything for this opportunity and want nothing more than to make something of myself without any help from my father.

Inside my purse, my phone pings with an incoming text.

Dean Brian Becker: Good luck today! Not that you need it. Don't forget the welcome faculty meeting later.

Me: Thank you. I'll be sure to be there after class.

I smile. The dean wishing me luck is like a good omen, right? I inhale deeply, taking in the scent of freshly cut grass and foliage, and begin to walk toward the student center where I'll grab a coffee in the café before I head to my office in Cameron Hall. There are students everywhere along the quad, young people milling about, catching up with friends and classmates, sitting on blankets on the grassy lawns or on benches with books. I fight the urge to smile again.

I'm a full-fledged assistant professor now. Bloody hell, I actually did it! On my own, I might add, without the help of my father, Dr. Andrew Phillip Butler.

Entering the commons building, I look down at my phone to find a few other text messages from Ana and a few friends from Boston all wishing me luck today. I begin to type out my response when I bump someone's shoulder.

An apology is just on my tongue when I look back to see the backs of two female students land their male friend walking out the door, just out of earshot.

A strange sense of déjà vu hits my senses. A memory of the man and the scent of his cologne brings back the reminder of my night spent with Hendy all those months ago. It's pathetic that I'm still thinking about this man, who is nowhere in the vicinity and has no reason to be on campus. He'd told me he was set to graduate from college last spring, so there's no way the man in line would've been him.

I shake off the ridiculous thought and head toward the very long coffee line.

This daydreaming about a man I had a one-night stand with over six months ago has got to stop. It's done, over, and I'll never see him again.

But that's easier said than done because that night had a searing effect on me. It was the best sex of my life, and despite the fact that we were perfect strangers, I felt a strong connection to him.

Hendy was funny, respectful, and insatiable. And while he was a few years younger than me, the age difference didn't bother me as much as I thought it would. The endurance and stamina he had from his youthful virility didn't hurt either.

"That's right, gorgeous. I'm going to make you come again, and again, and again..."

Someone from afar calls out, "Watch out!" and I duck just in time to avoid being pelted in the head with an incoming Frisbee. Another male voice yells, "Sorry!" and I give them a wave as I continue walking.

Pay attention, Charlotte, I chastise myself. Stop this excessive obsession over Hendy and his great sex skills and focus on the present.

As I walk into Cameron Hall, I click through today's agenda. I have several lectures to prep for, which means I need to get my head in the game.

Cameron Hall is where most of my lectures will be held and which also houses my office.

My office.

A jolt of excitement hits me in the gut, sending slivers of nerves through my bloodstream as I review my lecture notes and prepare my first presentation as an assistant professor.

"You can do this," I quietly encourage myself, with

more bravado than I actually feel. I gather up my things, lock my office door, and walk down to the small seminar room where I'll be teaching my first class of grad students today.

Making my way to the front of the classroom, I set down my laptop bag and coffee and peruse the roster of the fifteen students that are scheduled to be here today. Not nearly as daunting as a lecture hall full of over one hundred students like I used to teach back in my PhD days. Those were extremely nerve-racking, and it makes me even more grateful to be teaching at a small university and not a big one like in Boston.

Extracting my laptop from my bag, I set it on the podium and hook it up to the HDMI cord using the classroom's technology. With a deep breath, I hit a button and voilà, my slideshow appears on the screen.

Phew. Alright, at least I got that working. I'm concentrating on the curriculum when I hear a soft muffle of voices carrying down the stairs of the room as a few students begin filing in. I soon sense someone standing in front of me, and I look up to find a young man with dark auburn hair and a caterpillar mustache smiling at me.

"Hi, Professor Butler. I'm Chad Watkins," he greets me congenially. "I checked with the Registrar last week about adding your class and they said it's full. But would you mind if I audited today on the off-chance someone drops it?" His eyes and voice are full of hope. Poor guy. I'd hate to shatter it. I remember those days trying to play hopscotch in order to get in a class I needed to graduate.

"Sure, Chad. I can reach out to the dean and registrar's office, too, and see if we can't get you added. I know they like caps on the classes, but I hardly think sixteen people will break the system. I'm sure we have room," I say, offering him a warm smile and a gesture toward the room that can hold up to thirty. "But I'll let you know."

"Thanks, Professor. I really appreciate it," he says. "I'll just take a seat in the back."

I nod and a glow of pride covers my cheeks at the use of the term Professor as I watch him walk off to find a seat. I glance at the time on the clock and am about to start class and take roll call when my gaze scans over the room of bright-eyed students and lands on a familiar face.

I freeze.

I blink.

I nearly collapse.

Oh, no.

No, no, no.

This can't be happening.

This must be a hallucination or a figment of my imagination brought on by nerves. What else could explain the reason that Hendy is sitting in my classroom?

My heart hammers wildly in my chest as I stare in confused shock at Hendy, who doesn't seem to notice me because he's chatting with a girl sitting next to him.

Why the hell is he here in my class? When we met, he'd told me he would be graduating from college last spring. I never even thought to ask where he went to school, either. It seemed pointless considering I wasn't there to get to know him. He was simply going to fuck my brains out. And he did just that.

So I'm absolutely gobsmacked by this turn of events. This is madness.

My hot ski-vacation hookup is sitting in my seminar looking even better than he did six months ago.

He wears a black CFU Bears T-shirt that molds over his chest and biceps. A similarly embroidered hat sits low on his head, covering eyes that I know to be a brilliant blue. His square jawline is even more accentuated now with the lack of a beard and it makes him look even younger.

All my efforts to keep those memories of our night together fails and what he did to my body comes rushing back in a flood of senses.

His beard bristle tickles my lips as he presses his hot mouth to mine. Hot damn, this guy can kiss.

Our kiss goes from hot to scorching lava in under twenty seconds and I feel his hardened erection against my stomach when he presses me against the wall. His hand runs a calculated path over my clothed body and I reach up and slip my fingers through his hair.

"Too many clothes," he mumbles against my lips. I hum my agreement.

I'm not sure how we do it without breaking the kiss, but we each take off single items of clothes until we're both naked and panting. Then he takes a step back and his eyes drift over my body, devouring me with his hungry gaze.

"Fuck, you're gorgeous."

The flush that rises over my skin from those three simple words is my undoing. I lay back on the bed, spread my legs, and beckon him to crawl on top of me. His body is taut and firm and my hands roam with abandon, tracing the curves and valleys of this incredibly sexy man.

Not wanting to get too far ahead but knowing where this is going to lead, I manage to let a word escape my addled brain.

"Condom."

He frowns for a moment and then smirks a cheeky grin, nodding once before lifting himself from me and leaning down on the floor to fumble around for his pants. Yanking something from one of his pockets, he returns to my side, shaking a foil packet in his fingers like it's a prize.

"Quite the Boy Scout," I say with a raised eyebrow.

"Safety first, then fun," he replies with a wink, opening the packet with his teeth and rolling the condom over his impressive length. "Now, where was I?"

I sink back into the bed at the first touch of his fingers as they trace a seductive path up my thigh to find my swollen, wet flesh. He has me crying out within seconds, circling my clit and working me into a frenzy with his fingers before swiftly sinking into me as he skillfully brings me to orgasm.

"Don't stop!" I cry out as the edges of my vision darken as starlight explodes behind my eyelids. He doesn't and a moment after I fall into the bliss I so desperately needed, he follows suit and finds his own release.

I realize I've been holding my breath and staring into space when the sound of the classroom door slams and brings me back to reality. The entire room is now staring at me and I seem to return from another universe. I drag in some air to fill my lungs and try to calm myself before Hendy notices me standing in front of the room.

Then, as if he realizes the whole room has turned quiet, he slowly lifts his gaze, starting down at my feet and making his way up my body until our eyes meet and lock.

His face remains impassive, the only tell of recognition being the tip of his tongue making an arc around his mouth.

Bollocks. Fuck.

This is not what I expected on my first day of the semester.

I've never had a poker face, but maybe I can just ignore the fact that there is a conflict of interest in that I've already slept with one of my students.

Or maybe I'll get lucky and he'll drop this class. Yes, of course, why wouldn't he?

I'm sure he'll be unbearably uncomfortable sitting in my class day after day, week after week, and he'll not want the trouble.

A drop of sweat drips between my cleavage as dread washes over me. I swallow thickly, knowing I'm expected to address the class, but I'm not sure what I'm supposed to say.

With every ounce of wherewithal I can muster, I remind myself how to speak and begin my rehearsed speech.

"Good morning, everyone, and welcome. I'm Professor Charlotte Butler and this is Digital Marketing..." I stop suddenly, having drawn a complete blank and forgotten the course name.

Shit. Shit, shit, shit.

My prepared notes shake in my hand and I'm painfully aware of the snickers that waft around the room. A deep voice that sounds like it was forged in whiskey and cigarettes jumps in.

"Case Studies of European Countries."

I glance up, knowing exactly where it came from. "Thank you," I supply dully, trying to get my feet back underneath me.

"Yes, this is a graduate-level course, so if you're not a grad student or this isn't the class you enrolled in, now would be a great time to sneak out. I promise not to look."

I turn around, my back to the class, as my comment lightens the mood and laughter rises up. Then the shuffling of feet and the door opening and closing shut can be heard, letting me know at least one or more took me up on that offer.

Finally, I turn back around and grin.

"Happens every time," I add with a laugh. "Now, then. I'm excited to have you all here this semester. We'll dive into the lecture in a moment, but first, since we're a small class and we'll be doing a lot of group work over the next semester, I want to go around the room and introduce ourselves. If you could give me your full name so I may mark my attendance roster, where you're from, and your interest in the topic of our course, I would appreciate it."

I gesture to the student nearest me, a bright-eyed young woman with dark hair and eyes and an eager expression on her face.

"Would you care to begin?"

The student smiles and nearly jumps out of her chair to face the class.

"Hi. I'm Ellen Chang. I'm from Irvine, California. I want to be a marketing executive in my father's company once I've graduated with my MBA."

I smile politely at Ellen. "Thank you, Ellen. That's very admirable. Next?"

Another student rises and we continue to go through the room as I jot down their preferred pronouns and mark their presence on my roster, but my eyes continue to drift automatically to Hendy, who watches me with an intensity that is both thrilling and disorienting. Not once does he seem to give any notice to his classmates.

When it's finally his turn, his lips twitch in what we British term a cheeky grin.

"Good morning, *Professor* Butler," he drawls, drawing out my name. "I'm Joel Henderson, but everyone calls me Hendy."

Someone interrupts from behind with a, *"Go, Hendy!"* and my brows shoot up as I follow the sound with my gaze. When they return to Hendy...I mean...Joel...I mean, *ugh*...

Joel, er, Hendy laughs, glancing over his shoulder with a wave.

"Sorry, Professor. We have a lot of football fans on campus. I'm originally from Rivers Crossing, just twenty miles from here. I'm in this class because it's part of my graduate program." That crooked, sexy smile of his peeks out and my knees nearly buckle. "Lucky me, I hear you're the master on the topic."

I try not to blush as a few "*oohs*" fly around the room, which only makes my cheeks heat even hotter in this already warm room.

I force myself to nod and offer my brief response.

"Thank you, Joel. Next..."

My gaze shifts to the student next to him, who gives me her name, but to be honest, I still couldn't tell you what it was even if I were bound and tortured because I'm not listening.

The hungry perusal of my body by Hendy's eyes robs me of thought and common sense. I want to escape the scrutiny of his knowing glances, but I have to keep my composure and not let my knickers get in a twist.

When the last student finishes with their introduction, I return to my well-rehearsed lecture and work to keep my eyes off of Hendy.

By the end of the hour-long class, I'm feeling a bit more relaxed and my confidence has made a comeback.

The students file out of the classroom with their assignments for the next class and I return to the podium to turn off the projector and unplug my laptop, clearing my convoluted thoughts of the strange randomness that has occurred with the reemergence of my onetime lover. Poppy is going to have a heyday with this one.

No sooner have I finished packing up when I feel the

very heat of him next to me. I know it's him because I recognize his cedar and ocean scent before I even look up.

Slowly, I lift my gaze to the otherwise empty room, then turn to stare into familiar blue eyes.

"Fancy meeting you here, *Lottie*." He doesn't even try to hide his smirk. "I mean, Professor Butler."

I give him a pointed look. "Mr. Henderson, I think you and I should have a chat in my office. Immediately."

He presses his lips together and nods. "Absolutely. Lead the way. I'm all yours."

This time, I inhale deeply to indulge in the scent of his cologne thanks to his close proximity.

A proximity that I suspect will not change anytime in the near future because he'll be in my classroom.

Fuck. My. Life.

How do I get myself out of this clusterfuck of a mess?

Chapter Four

Hendy

Very few things or people in my life can catch me off guard and make me fumble, mostly because of my time playing football.

Over the years, beginning back in my peewee football league time, I've learned to employ my natural skills of reading people and their potential next moves. I've learned how to anticipate plays by judging the field positions so I could dodge and outrun, pivot, or dish the ball with a speed and grace few quarterbacks can muster.

My ability to adapt and remain flexible both on and off the field and in life is what makes me such a fucking great QB.

Or made me one. Past tense since I no longer play.

But *this* play wasn't listed in any of my playbooks or experiences with women.

There are no offensive plays or tricks to outmaneuver the quarterback sack I was just hit with when I walked in and saw that Lottie is my new professor.

I follow Lottie—or rather, Professor Butler—down the corridor and through the hallways filled with students, many of them calling out my name as we pass.

After the first few times, Lottie—*fuck*, I mean, Professor Butler—peers over her shoulder and gives me a cross between a glare and a look of confusion.

I shrug and continue on until she finally takes a sharp left down the main hallway toward the faculty lounge and offices.

It's quieter here and I'm enthralled with the sound of her high heels clicking against the shining wood floors. I stare at her toned legs...the ones that had been wrapped around my waist as I pounded into her during our one night together...and hell, I can't help the twitch in my pants as my dick stirs at the memories.

This whole thing is so surreal it's almost unbelievable. Like, if I told EJ and Killer about this strange reunion, they'd never believe it.

One minute I'm fucking a complete stranger on a ski vacation, with no idea of her full name or any life details, and six months later, here I am, one of her new students.

Jesus, what a mess.

Funny thing is, I remember all the drama that unfolded last year between Kelsie and Hayes when he showed up at our house party and she freaked out over being duped by him.

At the time, I didn't get it. So what? So he never told her he played football and was going to attend this school? Big fucking deal. Get over it.

But now I kind of get it.

Maybe I should be pissed at Lottie...and fuck it, I'm going to keep calling her that name in my head because that's who she is to me. She wasn't my professor or even Charlotte when we met. She was just Lottie and I got a *lottie* her between the legs.

I chuckle at my internal dialogue as she gives me an icy glare.

It's not surprising she seems a little pissed at the moment, too. She had no idea who I was when we slept together, either, and no way of knowing I'd be in one of her graduate classes this semester.

It's not something we discussed that night. Our one night wasn't anything like what Kelsie and Hayes had. They had a relationship, for fuck's sake. Lottie and I were just two consenting adults looking for a good time. And it was a fucking great time, if I do say so myself.

Lottie was the hottest lay I've ever had. I still think about her a lot when I'm alone and in bed. Or in the shower. Or just alone. My mind will wander back to our night together and my hand instinctively reaches for my hard cock. I bring myself to orgasm with thoughts of her audacious invitation to go to her place and fuck.

Was it more exciting because she's a few years older than me and I liked that I was more experienced than her in bed?

Was it her smokin' hot body and the legs that didn't quit?

Or those low sexy moans and the whimpers she made when I was between her legs, and the way she asked for *more, more, more* in that seductive British accent?

Jesus, I had a hard on for this woman for weeks after our hookup and my dreams were taken over with images of her gorgeous fucking mouth wrapped around my cock.

I swallow and discreetly adjust my now tight jeans as we get to the door of her office. I wait patiently while she unlocks the door, opens it, and reaches to flip on the light. The move only serves to increase the lust that threatens to overtake me when I breathe in her lemony sugar scent.

Barely three inches separate us. If things were different, I could close the door behind us, press her against the wall, cup her cheek, and kiss the living hell out of her.

But that's not happening now. Our weird turn of events won't allow me to live out my fantasy of fucking my new professor on her desk.

Instead, I make myself take a step back and watch as she rounds the edge of her neatly organized desk. She sits down and, for a moment, drops her head in what looks to be defeated contemplation. When she lifts her gaze again, her eyes bore into me. Not in fiery passion like the last time we were together, but in grave earnestness.

"Joel..."

"Hendy," I correct, my brows lifting upward and a smirk forming on my mouth. I like this side of her—the professional.

As if to prove she will not give in to my overt flirting, she starts again, leaning forward over her desk, her cream blouse tightening over her breasts, a resolute look in her expression.

"*Mr. Henderson.* This unforeseen and obviously uncomfortable situation we seem to have found ourselves in is quite serious. It creates a multitude of problems for me. For you."

I take a seat across from her desk and drop my bag on the floor next to the chair and casually crossing my leg over my knee, placing my elbows on the chair arms.

"I disagree, *Professor.* I don't know what problem you're referring to. I have no problem at all." I lay it on thick, doing my best to ruffle the feathers of this beautiful bombshell professor. "I'm not uncomfortable at all."

Everything about that night comes rushing back so clearly in the moment. The way she melted under the first brush of my knuckles across her cheek and the hot kiss out by our cars. How she quivered when my mouth was between her legs. The bite of her fingernails as they scored down my back.

Yeah, it's going to be a fun semester.

She inhales deeply and huffs out a breath of air, clearly not on the same page.

"Yes, Joel. There *is* a problem. One that could be utterly damaging to my career if anything about our shared time together gets out." She presses her lips together, the frown marring her perfect features, and anchors me hard with her green eyes.

"It can never get out. Do you understand me?"

Lottie pauses a moment and places her hands demurely in her lap. It's clearly obvious she is not originally from the US with her straight-spined, debutante stature. If someone were to tell me she came from old money and was of royal descent, I wouldn't bat an eye. She's absolutely regal with that tight bun sitting low at her neck, a braid of hair elegantly wrapped over the top of her head like a goddamn crown.

Her bright green eyes flash with anger and she levels me with a pointed stare. A shaky hiss of breath passes through her lips.

"Here's what's going to happen," she says with authority. "You're going to talk to the registrar to drop this class immediately, and we will do our very best to ignore each other on campus."

I screw up my nose and tilt my head to the side, as if debating the merits of her request.

"No can do, Prof," I state mildly but with a forceful shake of my head. She can't hide the shock on her face, no matter how stoic she tries to be or whether she might typically be the '*keep calm and carry on*' type.

"This is a required class in my program and my schedule is locked in tight so I can finish with my master's degree this year."

Her expression morphs into something I can't read and I scoot forward in my seat, placing my hands on top of her desk.

In a deep, daring voice, I murmur the next words in a raspy whisper.

"Here's what's actually going to happen, *Lottie*...I'm not going to drop your class." I pause for good measure. Her eyes flare at my rebellious response. "During this semester, every time I'm in your classroom, during every lecture you facilitate and seminar you lead, I will be a good student and dutifully take my notes and listen to you speak, participating in all the important discussions, completing all the required assignments on time. But all the while..."

I cock my head to the side and raise my eyebrows. "I will be imagining you just as you were six months ago...on your knees in front of me, getting me off with your mouth."

The statement is crass. It's over the line. It's inappropriate. It begs for a reaction.

A reaction that comes in the form of a loud gasp and causes angry blotches of red color her otherwise creamy white neck and cheeks. Or she could be turned on, I don't know. But I like it.

Without waiting for any further argument, I grab my bag and stand from the seat, walking toward the door.

As I turn the knob, I peer over my shoulder one last time to see Lottie appraising me candidly.

"Joel," she says in a whispered plea, a long, slender hand coming to clutch at her pretty neck. "Please don't let me regret that night."

"My only regret now is that it wasn't longer."

My wink is the last thing she sees when I close the door quietly behind me.

Then I hear a noise that sounds like books crashing against the door and I chuckle.

Oh yeah. It's going to be an interesting semester.

Chapter Five

Charlotte

That little shit.

That goddamn cocky little shit!

Okay, he's not little at all, but damn him! Damn the whole universe!

I look down at the books now scattered across my office floor and heave a dramatic sigh. I have never let my anger get the best of me or let it get physical. I am, after all, my father's daughter. We British are notoriously and stereotypically stoic in nature.

Why am I letting this man...this *student* get to me?

Oh yeah, because I let his penis get inside me.

"Unknowingly," I mutter to myself, as if I'm trying to explain it all away. I begin picking up and restacking the books I threw on the corner of my desk. A curse rips from under my breath as I notice a page ripped from one.

After placing the last book on my desk, I walk over to my chair, slumping into it and dropping my head in my hands. Half of me wants to believe this is all a bad dream, that when I uncover my eyes, I'll be back in my bed and none of this would have ever happened.

The other half of me...my traitorous body...well, it's happy as hell that the man who gave me the best night of sex ever just showed back up in my life.

"You're going to get us sacked, you cunt," I grumble, glancing down at myself to see the skin of my chest still splattered with red blotches. It's my telltale sign that, as a redhead, I can never hide my feelings when I'm frustrated or angry.

Now that I'm a professor, I need to do a better job of controlling those feelings, especially where Hendy is involved.

Involved. That word could easily be used if anyone ever finds out about us. They'd assume we're involved now, even though that's farthest from the truth.

It will never happen again, despite the erotic images Joel painted for me about what he'd be thinking during every class. Despite not knowing who I was when we slept together, now that he knows I'm his professor, Joel now probably sees me as a challenge. Like some kind of conquest, trying to bang his older professor again.

His words come streaming back to me.

Jesus, that was so hot. Logically, I know I shouldn't have liked it. It should've been offensive that he used such inappropriate language, and I should have admonished him.

But I wasn't offended at all. Something about his suggestion of *control* turned me on. The thing is, I hate being controlled. It's the reason why I left England.

Yet, here I am, my pussy throbbing in that needy way

because of how Joel described his fantasy of me dropping to my knees and using my mouth again to get himself off.

I run a frustrated hand through the hair in my bun and yank it undone with a tiny growl, letting my hair cascade loosely over my shoulders.

What is wrong with me? It's my first day in my new academic role and I'm getting overheated by the demanding and direct words of my student.

My mind drifts back unbidden to my ex-boyfriend, Oliver. He was everything my family thought was boyfriend material. Slightly older, well-established, and the soon-to-be head of a financial consulting firm in London. He was also a favorite lecturer at the Saïd Business School at the University of Oxford, which was seen as a highly respectable position to my parents.

But behind closed doors, Oliver was controlling and verbally abusive. After a childhood with my father, who was similar in nature, I'd become thick-skinned and adept at letting his verbal insults go. But after an event one night where he drank too much and forcefully grabbed my arm during an argument, I left him. I went to Poppy's flat and applied to four PhD programs in the United States. I was accepted within three months and left a few months after that.

I have learned through exerting my independence that I don't ever want to be treated disrespectfully or in a controlling manner ever again.

An inner rage begins to bubble to the surface once more. I won't be seen as weak. Especially weak over a man. Never again.

A knock at my door startles me and breaks me away from my convoluted thoughts. I quickly straighten my blouse and glance at the handheld mirror in my desk drawer, wiping away a smudge of mascara before answering. Did Joel return to apologize? To tell me he's dropping the class after all?

"Come in," I state authoritatively.

The door opens and I'm shocked to see Hubert Collingsworth, a colleague of my father's and an old family friend back in England.

"Hubert?" I say, completely surprised by his out-of-the-blue appearance in my office. Apparently, today is the day of reconnecting with unexpected acquaintances.

Hubert is one of the good ones. He's kind and generous with his time, and nearing retirement age. His wife passed away a few years ago, leaving him widowed with time on his hands that he now spends traveling the world visiting family and friends, as well as guest lecturing at prestigious universities. Hubert reminds me of my own grandfather who died when I was young, and I have a soft spot for him in my heart.

"Hello, Charlotte darling. How is my favorite new professor?" he asks exuberantly as he walks over to where I now stand in shock, offering me a fatherly kiss on my cheek.

I throw my arms around him in a big hug and when I step back, I look at him in confusion. "What in the world are you doing here?"

He gives a small chuckle. "I was speaking with your father and he told me you recently joined the faculty at Clearview Falls. I just happened to have a speaking engagement not far from here this week, so why not pop by and see if I could steal you away for a pint?" he explains, giving me his mustached, warm smile.

"Oh, of course, I'd love to," I offer, peeking at my watch to check the time. "But I do have other classes and a faculty meeting today. Could we meet up tomorrow evening?"

"Wonderful," he replies, clasping his hands together firmly. "I'll look forward to it. I've been told there's a good pub just off campus called The Bear Paw. Shall we say six tomorrow evening?"

"That would be lovely. Do you know your way around campus or do you need directions?"

Hubert waves me off with a gesture toward the door as I grab my materials for my next class. "I'll get directions from the hotel concierge. Don't you worry about me."

I open the door and Hubert follows me out of the office and down the hallway. Students trickle by on their way to their next classes or other activities, and it gives me a renewed rush of excitement for the term ahead.

As we reach my classroom door, I say my goodbyes.

"Now off you go and have a good class, Professor." Hubert gives me another peck on my cheek and then turns to head off in the direction of the student union.

I watch him amble off and shake my head at the strange morning I've had already. First Hendy and now Hubert.

Two blasts from my past and one of them an unwelcome one.

The next day my two lectures go rather smoothly and I use the remaining time to focus on my lecture notes for tomorrow. In a blink of an eye, the day is over and I meet up with Hubert at the Bear Paw pub just a block off campus.

We'd decided on two pints of lager and toast to one another. A sense of homesickness washes over me as I sit across from my family friend. The beer, the pub, the accent all remind me of home.

"So tell me all about your courses, my darling Charlotte."

I take my first sip, toss away that blue feeling, and begin to tell him about my courses and curriculum.

"I've been tasked with teaching a small seminar on Mondays and Wednesdays and two lectures on Tuesdays and Thursdays. I'm also currently working on a paper that I'd like to finish writing and have published in the spring."

"Sounds lovely. You've always been such an over-achiever that I have no doubt you will do what you say you'll do." I blush under Hubert's compliment.

It's so rare that I hear high praise from senior figures. My father has never complimented me for my achieve-ments. Overachieving was simply a nonnegotiable with him. Yet even earning the highest marks were still never enough to make him proud of me.

As if reading my thoughts, Hubert continues.

"I haven't seen your father since before the holidays." He scratches the bald spot on his head, as if puzzling out an invisible calendar in his brain. Then he shakes off the thought. "We keep missing one another. Andrew continues to be at the top of his game. There's no slowing him down. I think the apple doesn't fall from the tree." He raises his bushy eyebrows dubiously.

"Oh, I don't know about that," I say, thinking how vastly different I am from my father. "From what I hear, my father is doing fine."

Our conversation continues as Hubert shares news from home and I fill him in on my recent life updates and we order and finish our dinners, including a second round of drinks.

Finally, a waitress returns to our table to check on us.

"Another round for either of you?"

"None for this old man. How about you, Charlotte?" Hubert replies, glancing over at me.

I shake my head and pat my very full stomach. "I'm stuffed, thank you. Just a box for takeaway, please." I motion to my unfinished burger, and she nods and walks off toward the bar.

It's been nice to catch up with Hubert, but our conversation has made me a tad antsy. I want to be home to mentally prep for the fact that I'll be seeing Hendy in class tomorrow. That is, if he stays true to his firm commitment to remain in my class. When I checked the enrollment system earlier today, his name was still listed on the roster.

Just my luck. My one-night stand that won't leave.

We chitchat a bit more until Hubert calls it a night. He places some bills on the table and we stand to give each other hugs.

"Thank you so much for dinner and the company. It was so nice to see you."

"The pleasure was all mine, pet." He boops me on the tip of my nose as if I'm still a little girl. And just as he grabs his hat to place it on his head, he brings up the one subject I didn't want to discuss.

"By the way, I just ran into Oliver at a reception I attended a fortnight ago. He inquired about you and your whereabouts." I step back, wobbling a bit on my heels and grab the back of the chair to remain upright. Here we go.

"Oh?" I try to keep the disdain out of my voice. "What did you tell him?"

"He asked if I'd heard from you lately. I told him no but that I might be over in the States and would see you. He prattled on and on about you and asked that I pass on his regards. Oliver sure does seem to miss you." He eyes up my reaction and I think he wants to know how I am post-breakup, even though it feels like a lifetime ago. I know my parents still hope I'll forgive Oliver and come back home someday. That will never happen.

I shrug. "Well, I'm sure he'll find someone new soon. I've found that I enjoy being on my own for once."

And not being controlled by a man who thinks he owns me, I think to myself.

He nods. "Good for you, pet. I need to get going, but it was such a pleasure to spend time with you. Thanks for indulging this old man with your lovely conversation."

I smile and lean in for a proper hug, wishing my parents were more like Hubert. He clearly saw I didn't want to talk about Oliver and dropped the questions.

He kisses my cheek. "Right, then. Good night, Charlotte."

I smile as he leaves and then sit back down to wait for the waitress to return with my box, using the time to think through the last part of our conversation.

I thought I was doing well and had come so far in getting over Oliver. But his name dredges up all those old feelings I've tried to bury and move on from.

That incredible one-night with Joel had given me the morale boost I needed to push forward in my life and forget about the messy breakup with Oliver.

In fact, that one-night stand made me realize something I never knew about myself when I was with Oliver: I can orgasm with a man and I like being told what to do in bed.

I flush at the thought just as two beers and a box are set down on my table. I blink and stare up at the waitress.

"I didn't order any more beer. I only wanted the box," I insist, but she throws a look over her shoulder toward the bar and then shoots me a grin.

"They're from Hendy."

Chapter Six

H endy

I slide off my barstool and slip a twenty-dollar bill into Cassie's hand as she walks past me. She gives me a side-eye glance and mutters, "Go get her, QB." Then I take a seat at the table opposite of Lottie as she stares incredulously at me.

"I can help you drain those," I offer with a quirk of my brow, gesturing with a finger to the beers. "Having a nice night, Professor?"

She frowns at me and I stare into her gorgeous green eyes, her reddish-gold hair glowing even in the dim bar lights. I swear the air crackles with the electricity between us.

Fuck me. This night would be better if I could run my hands through her hair and over her curves.

This attraction to Lottie is extremely inconvenient

and one I can't seem to shake. I understand her reasons for wanting me to stay away and to steer clear of any potential rumors between us, but how can I do that when she is so goddamn beautiful? And it's not just that. This thing between us feels like an invisible force stronger than any magnet on the planet pulling us together despite the odds.

"I was having a good evening, thanks for asking," she murmurs, folding her hands together on the table. "Until you showed up."

I make a tsking noise and slide the invitingly frothy beer toward her, hoping to persuade her to stay for a drink.

When I showed up at the bar tonight, it was for the sole purpose of meeting up with a few of my old teammates to play some darts and pool since we don't have any games to watch yet. Under normal circumstances, I'd be out with my crew, but now that EJ and Killer are graduated and gone, and Lucy, Grace, and Kelsie are busy with school, I don't have anyone to hang with.

So I came early to have dinner and do a bit of homework while I waited for Mac and my other dudes. I had a spot at the bar and was watching the big screen TV when I heard Lottie's voice from behind me. Before I even turned around, I knew it was her. My confusion, however, stemmed from the old man she was talking with.

Is he her father? Her boyfriend? Jesus, I hope not.

Lottie is far too young to be dating a guy that age. There had to be a thirty-year age difference between them. Almost as wide as the age difference between Bill Belichick and his girlfriend. I'm all about loving who you want, but dating someone old enough to be your grandparent? That's where I draw the line.

It makes me wonder exactly how old Lottie is? I stare at

her pale, smooth complexion and the soft curve of her cheekbones. She can't be over thirty.

"Who was the dude you were with?" I keep my voice neutral, but I'm feeling a bit proprietary, which is lame because I have no claim to her. No right to even ask.

But I do anyway.

Lottie narrows her eyes and puckers her lips. "None of your business."

I laugh it off, knowing she's right.

"I think we need to talk," I say, fighting back a suggestive smile. She drags the pint glass toward her and then brings it to her lips. The creamy foam dots the top of her full mouth, but she swipes it away before I can lift a finger to do the honors for her.

"You should schedule an appointment during office hours like all my other students."

Laughter trickles out of my mouth and I tip my head to the side, a cocky smile forming on my lips. "I think we can both agree I'm a little *different* from your *other* students."

Despite the lighting, I can see the blush that blooms over her creamy white cheeks and her expression tells me she wants to smack me. Or maybe even smack my ass.

Hmm...that'd be fun.

Her eyes dart away as if she might even be thinking the same thing and she takes a long pull of the beer. The night we met, she ordered wine. I like the fact that she can drink a beer just as well and isn't a hoity-toity wine snob.

Although, it wouldn't matter. If she even hinted at the idea that she wanted me to take her back to her place to fuck her right now, I'd do it in a second. I'm horny as fuck and haven't been laid in...well...a long time. I'd like to say it was just a dry spell, but I'm pretty sure that's not it.

I've been hung up on someone else.

And that someone is sitting across from me right now, drinking a beer and shooting me daggers with her eyes. But a man's gotta try.

I down the rest of my beer, needing to quench my dry throat after that thought.

"So you won't tell me who the old guy was?"

"Sod off, Joel, or Hendy, whatever your name is," she protests, using the British slang that only intensifies when she's a little miffed. It also increases her hotness by another fifty degrees. "I don't need to explain myself to you, but he's an old family friend and he's in town as a guest lecturer in the economics department."

"Good," I reply. "Under normal circumstances, I like a bit of healthy competition. But in your case, I don't want to compete."

She sniffs. "Compete for what, exactly?"

"You."

A very unladylike grunt barrels from her mouth. "Excuse me? Get that out of your head right now. We are not going there again."

I lean over the table and speak softly so as not to be overheard—especially by Cassie, who is a total gossip—but firmly. "By going there, do you mean between your legs?"

"Oh my God!" Lottie rises from her seat, swaying unsteadily on her feet, and lifts her hand at me in protest. She jabs a finger in the air. "You can't say things like that to me, Hendy. Ever again. I need to leave."

I jump up and reach for her waist because she looks like she could topple over—either from too much to drink or her flustered indignation. "Whoa there, Lottie. I've got you."

"It's *Professor* Butler to you, Hendy," she hisses out in a slightly slurred accent. "And I am quite capable of standing on my own. Now, let go of me. I don't need your help."

She wrenches herself free, grabs her purse from the back of the chair—which gets stuck, causing her to curse out a mumbled *bugger* and yank the strap free—and starts toward the exit.

I follow along behind her as we head through the crowded room, ready to help her at a moment's notice if she stumbles.

"You're not driving, right?"

She pushes out the door and then glares back at me.

"I'm walking home, thank you very much."

I nod and take my place next to her, not saying another word.

She stops after a few steps and lets out an exasperated sigh.

"Joel, what do you think you're doing?"

"I'm walking you home. Obvs." I smile in the dark because she makes a little angry growl sound.

For reasons unbeknownst to me, Lottie suddenly begins to laugh. Side-splitting, bent-over, hysterical laughter like what I just said is the funniest thing she's ever heard. I know she's had a few beers, but I didn't think she was that drunk.

I lay a hand on her back and she pops back up to a stand, her laughter turning to a hiccup and then a slight grumble of protest.

And then, in a sudden and unexpected move, Lottie turns to face me, grabs hold of my shirt in her hand, and crushes her lips to mine.

It takes me a millisecond to formulate a thought, but when I do, that thought is all about getting this woman into my bed again.

I need it. I need *her*. In a way I've never needed a woman before.

Swinging an arm around her lower back, I guide her

backward to the corner of the building, away from prying eyes, and press her against the wall, never once letting my lips leave hers.

She is wild and frenzied, her hands roaming my backside, nails scoring over my clothes as if she's determined to tear them from my body.

This is dangerous. I know the risks involved and so does she. But the threat holds no merit at this moment because everything is about getting Lottie naked and inside her body.

My blood pulses through my cock, my erection wedged between her legs and my arms cage her against the exterior building wall. From this location, no one can see us unless one of the pub employees comes out to the side alley for a smoke.

I let my hands wander up her sides, one hand snaking under her shirt to find her breast. Her nipple hardens under the pad of my thumb and she moans into my mouth.

"I want to spread you out naked on my bed and fuck these perfect tits."

Lottie squirms against me, creating a frantic friction as she grinds her pussy over my hard cock. This time it's me who groans.

"Are you wet for me, Professor?"

She gasps when my hand tunnels under her waistband and I deftly undo her pants. I slide my fingers through the soft curls, then dip inside her heat.

"Yes," she murmurs, clasping her fingers in my hair.

"So fucking wet."

The sound of a car door slamming and voices and laughter from the parking lot pull us out of our sexual haze, and I reluctantly drag my hand from her pants. But I don't want to lose this connection, so I press my mouth to the dip in her neck and suck greedily at her skin.

"I think you need to be taught a lesson," Lottie says suddenly, her voice husky with need. "One more time. That's it. No more."

She tugs my hoodie over my head to shield my face, grabs my hand, and guides me out to the sidewalk as we head off into what I presume is the direction of her house.

I'll take anything to get Lottie in bed again.

I can accept just one more night, I tell myself.

But that's a lie.

Because the truth is, I'll never stop wanting her. Even if she is my professor.

Chapter Seven

C harlotte

It's the heat that wakes me. I'm so bloody hot.

I reach out to throw off the blankets...and then remember.

What the fucking hell did I do?

I slowly open an eye to find myself sprawled across Hendy. My face rests on his chest and his arm is slung around my back. And I'm pretty sure his erection is digging into my leg that is somehow over the top of his muscular thigh, the soft hairs covering it tickling my skin.

I listen to the sound of his steady breathing, the gentle rise and fall of his chest. It seems he's still in a deep sleep, which means I have a chance of sneaking out of bed without notice if I can carefully peel myself off of him.

I make small, minuscule movements to extricate myself from the heat of his body inch by inch, stopping several times when the tempo of his breath changes. He mumbles something incoherently as he shifts to his back, and I am able to free myself completely. His head lolls to the side, and his breath turns into a light snore.

Okay, now is my chance to gather up my clothes and leave, putting distance between what happened with us last night.

I pause to pick up my panties from the floor, then realize my foolishness.

This is my room--in my house--*dammit*! I can't do the walk of shame from my own home.

I drop the panties and cover my face with my hands, disgusted with myself for my lack of self-control.

It wasn't alcohol intoxication that had me making this stupid decision. I wasn't pissed enough from the beer I consumed to lose my faculties to consent to sleep with Joel.

Oh no. I slept with Joel because I wanted to. Plain and simple. My body took over the minute he gave me that cocky-assured smile of his across the pub table.

And then what?

Oh yeah, I practically launched myself at him and then brought him back here.

Memories suddenly return to me like little kernels of popcorn popping in my brain.

The laughter that bubbled up inside of me as we left the pub and the moment I decided to say, *fuck it* and throw caution to the wind, kissing him in a parking lot where anyone could've seen us.

The feeling of Joel's skilled fingers slowly sliding my panties down my legs and his lips trailing up the sensitive flesh of my inner thigh, his tongue and fingers slipping inside my wet heat and then pumping languidly as he sucked on my clit.

And lest I not forget, that instant when he flipped me over onto my stomach and slammed inside of me, thrusting so deep that I nearly saw stars and then did see them when he played my swollen bundle of nerves like a musical instrument. Especially when he pulled me over his face and lapped at my pussy like I was the best thing he'd ever had.

Damn him.

He's the best lover I've ever been with. The sex last night was even better than I remember from the ski trip.

He's in a league all his own.

Whether it's from the stamina gained from playing football or just his youthful virility this man does things to me that no one has ever done, taking me to the precipice and back again, over and over, until I am a limp noodle.

The man gifted me with multiple orgasms using his tongue and fingers and that was before his very impressive dick even got involved. It's very well possible Joel Henderson has a magic cock.

Speaking of which. I glance down at the tented sheet covering his morning wood. There's an irrational part of me that wants to take him in my mouth and let him fuck my face until I'm swallowing his release down my throat. Or maybe he'd yank me off my knees before he comes, toss me on the bed and then thrust into me while holding my legs wide, just like he did last night.

Fuck, that was so hot.

Why did sex with him have to be so good? Is it because he's absolutely off-limits to me? Or perhaps because I secretly love that he's younger and I find that sexy?

Joel is literally the whole package. He's the type of man I dream of meeting—cockiness and all. It's that component that makes him seriously hot.

Stop calling him hot, I chastise myself, slipping on yoga

pants and a T-shirt and leaving the room to go in search of my trainers.

I'll go get some coffee and clear my head. Give myself some space away from his sexy pheromones that obviously make me a total twat.

With no lectures on my schedule this morning, I'd been planning on spending this morning holed up in my office to work on my research paper, yet here I am, arguing with myself over the conundrum I've put myself in.

I finish lacing my shoes when, as if on cue, the sound of the toilet flushing draws my attention to my bedroom door. A moment later, Joel stands in front of me in nothing but his jeans. My hungry gaze zeros in on the "V" of muscle tapering low, covered with a thatch of dark hair disappearing into the waistband. The terrain my tongue explored last night. My mouth salivates.

His thumb loops in that waistband and he leans his shoulder into the door jamb. The action tugs his jeans further and skyrockets his sexy meter up from a hundred to a thousand. He smirks at me knowingly and I look back down to my shoes.

"See anything of interest, Professor?" he teases.

I practically growl. "No. In fact, I need to go. I have a conference call in a bit. I need to leave. Feel free to have a coffee," I say and haphazardly motion to the one-cup coffee maker sitting on my counter.

"Okaaay..." An eyebrow quirks up suspiciously. "And you're going to go on to campus in running clothes?"

I glance down at my choice of clothing and grimace. I've obviously been caught in a lie but now it's too late.

"It's just a call." I wave my hand and stand up, turning toward the door.

He snickers and grabs the T-shirt he threw on my couch

last night, pulling it over his head, and slips into his shoes. "Well, let me walk you."

"No, it's fine," I blurt out quickly, probably too quickly. "I need time to think...alone...about my research paper."

I don't even say goodbye, I just start running the minute I'm off my front porch, hoping he won't follow me but secretly wishing he would.

Gah. What is wrong with me? I'm giving myself mental whiplash over these feelings I have for Joel. I cannot in good conscience see him outside of class and then, once the semester is over, we won't ever need to speak again.

My mind flashes back to the way his tongue swirled around my nipples last night and I groan to myself. Who am I kidding? This man is my kryptonite. How in the hell am I going to be able to stay away from him?

My phone is in hand and my earbuds in, so I call the one person who can talk some sanity into me.

"Poppy?" I say as she answers.

"Are you dead?" she asks.

"I'm literally calling you, so no," I grumble. Sometimes Poppy's sarcasm can reach levels that almost annoy me. Only sometimes. Like now, when I'm madder than a hatter at myself for falling back into bed with my student.

Oh, Sweet Jesus. I am such a stupid twat.

"Why are you a twat?" Her voice interjects over my self-flagellation. "I'd call you more of a wench."

Shit, I said that out loud.

"Piss off," I say. Her cackling laughter burns a hole in my ear. I stop and bend over at the waist, placing one hand on my hip, and take a fortifying gulp of air. "I need you to talk some sense into me and tell me to act like an adult."

She's quiet for a beat. "You didn't call Oliver in a moment of loneliness, did you?"

"No, absolutely not!"

"Okay, well, it can't be worse than that," she says matter-of-factly. "So, what is it? Who'd you sleep with? And was it good?"

"Oh. My. God… so good," I respond pitifully.

She laughs and I roll my eyes. As much as Poppy wants me to have fun, she also knows how much this job means to me.

"I slept with Joel again."

Dead silence.

This time the pause is more than a beat. I hear her suck in a breath.

"I'm sorry…what did you say? I think I just heard that you slept with your student again?"

After the first day of classes, I'd called Poppy and told her about the whole sordid ordeal. How I called him into my office afterward and laid down the law and how he willfully ignored it.

"I met with Hubert last night at a local pub and Joel showed up and then one thing led to another and suddenly I was kissing him and I brought him home," I finish in one long breath.

"Let me see if I got this straight. You fucked a rando on a ski trip last spring. Then, that rando turns out to be one of your grad students, who you've expressly forbidden yourself to interact with outside of class, and then you fucked him again last night?" she recounts incredulously. "Is that correct, Professor Butler?"

I mentally flip my best friend off but grant her the acknowledgment. "Yes, you are correct. It was a complete mistake," I reply as I stop in front of a bench and plop down on it. I lower my head into my free hand and twirl the lanyard with my campus ID and key ring around my thumb.

"I regret I made a horrible and irresponsible decision and it will never happen again."

Even as I say the words, I wonder how I'll manage to keep this promise to myself and to Poppy when I'm face-to-face with him every week inside my classroom for the remainder of the semester?

"That's so hot," she answers, choosing to ignore my need for counseling advice. "And also really fucked up. I'm so proud of you, Lots!"

I heave a sigh of exasperation. "Damn you, Pop. Don't be proud. Be disgusted. This is a complete clusterfuck made of my own bad decision-making and I'm not sure how to reverse the effects." I run my hand through my hair, a mess of a reddish crow's nest that I'll need to wash before my next meeting.

"So, just tell him you'll fail him," she suggests breezily, as if that's the ethical answer to this unethical problem. "He's probably a moron, anyway, being that he played American football."

A few students pass by me on the pathway and I wait until they're out of earshot to speak again.

"That's not ethical, you know," I whisper. I can't do that to him if he does the work. I will not let my personal feelings color my role in academia.

She blows out what I assume is smoke from the cigarette she still smokes. "Then threaten to go to the dean and acknowledge the past affair."

"Fuck no!" I yelp and cover my mouth, glancing around surreptitiously to make sure no one heard that. I lower my voice. "What if Joel retaliates and does that to *me*?"

"Hmmm...well, I don't know. Do you like him?" I can hear the gravitas in her voice and know the question is sincere.

"It doesn't matter. I'm not risking everything I worked for, not for anyone," I say with an air of sadness.

"Okay, I guess that settles it then. Move on and upwards. By the way, what's Hubert doing out there?" Poppy asks, completely catching me off guard.

"He was a guest lecturer. And..." I trail off, considering her other question. *Do I like Joel?* Yes. I really do like him. At some point last night, in between rounds of incredible sex, he pulled a Charles Dickens book off my nightstand and started quoting from it, from memory and then gave me an opinion on the theme. It turns out the football player is very smart. I suppose it makes sense since he's in a grad school program.

"And yes, I like Joel. There, I said it. If I weren't his professor, I'd want to see more of him. Ugh. Why does this have to be so complicated, Pop?"

"Complications aside, I think you have your answer," she says. "You little slag, you."

I huff with indignation. "I am *not* a slag."

Oops. I may have said that a bit too loud because a pair of female students walk by, whip their heads in my direction, and giggle as they walk on. *Shit.* I can't be caught cursing and swearing like a sailor around students.

Just then my phone buzzes with an incoming text from an unknown number. I pull my phone away from my ear and click on it.

Unknown: Coffee is good...but it'd be better in bed, naked with you.

Shit, it's Joel. I forgot I gave my students my mobile number so they could contact me with any questions during the semester. My cheeks flush and a pang of lust hits me in the center of my legs.

"Lottie? What's happening?"

"He just texted me," I state dryly, taking a screenshot to send her. "It's what I feared…he's not going to give this up."

It's obvious when she sees the text because she whistles. "Hot damn. I like his vibe."

"Poppy! Focus!" I chastise, wondering if I'll even get good advice from her at this point or if she's just going to keep pushing me toward Joel.

Poppy has been known to give me very good advice when I've needed it. After all, she was the one who talked me into leaving Oliver and coming to the US, the best decision I could have ever made.

But she seems a bit hung up on me pursuing this thing with Joel.

"Well, you have two choices," she asserts. "You can report it to the dean and hope there are no repercussions, or you keep having amazing sex with your student on the down-low, in a clandestine affair."

"I don't like either option," I admit, even though the second option sounds very tantalizing probably because it's forbidden.

"Okay, then maybe tell him you're going to divulge it to the dean and see what Joel says. It could push him to decide to drop your class after all."

I consider the merits of this action. It's not the worst idea.

"Okay. I'll give that a try. Can't hurt," I agree.

Or it could sting like a sonofabitch.

We say our goodbyes and I text Joel back with my reply.

Me: This ends now. Please stop with the suggestive flirting. I'm going to talk to the dean tomorrow.

There's an immediate response.

Unknown: I see. Well, that's bad.

Unknown: And you know that bad girls get spanked, don't they?

Unknown: Oops. Sorry. Was that suggestive, Professor?

Unknown: I guess that means we have one more night to be bad together.

Damn him. He went in for the kill shot.

His dirty talk is a huge turn-on. Maybe I have a kink and never knew it until Joel showed up in my life.

And maybe this forbidden game of rule-breaking that I'm playing with him is what has me excited about something, or someone, for the first time in a very long time.

I love a good game.

Chapter Eight

H endy

My classes are done for the day and I'm bored as fuck.

In the past, I would have had football practice or strength training or meetings with the coaches to occupy my time. Then in the evenings, I'd do homework and hang out with the guys to chill and game together.

But now they're both gone and living their lives in their new careers.

I walk through campus and am ready to head home when my feet automatically veer toward the field house and the stadium. It may make me a glutton for punishment, but I want to see what's going on with the team.

Entering the side door, I give a nod to Dexter, the security guard, who pumps a fist in the air as I walk by.

"Good to see you, Hendy," he says in his booming baritone voice. "You coming to give the team a pep talk?"

I chuckle because I'm anything but peppy these days and would be no good at motivating anyone, much less myself.

"'Sup, man? Nah, I'm just checking in to see what's what," I offer noncommittally. "Maybe I'll watch a bit of practice."

He nods. "They're not looking as good as they used to. They sure could use your leadership on the field again."

Talk about a dagger to the heart. Damn, that hits hard.

I give him a wave. "Thanks. See ya later, Dex."

I breathe in the air within the corridor, the scent thick with sweat and dirt, but it brings with it a flood of nostalgia and memories. Good times that I miss more than I care to admit. I head down the hall toward the building exit that leads out to the field.

A few more steps and I'm passing Coach Brewster's door, which is open, and the light is on. I'm surprised to see him sitting at his desk with his head bowed forward propped in his hands. My first instinct is to say hi, but it looks like he's either concentrating on something big or he has a headache. In either case, I'm not about to disturb him, especially since I have no reason to be here. I quietly walk past the door, leaving him without interruption, when suddenly he calls out to me.

"QB One, is that you?" he asks in his usual brusque voice. I stop in my tracks and peer my head around the doorframe. Coach's head is now cocked to the side and a strange look is on his face. "Get your ass in here, Hendy."

I do as he says—because no one ever dares to contradict Coach, even if I'm no longer one of his players—and stride inside, where I stop behind one of his desk chairs.

"Hey, Coach. I was just going to—"

He interrupts me without apology. "You're just the man I needed to see. Take a seat."

Coach waves me toward the chair and, confused at his comment, I do as he says and plop my ass down on the seat. I place my backpack near my feet and check my posture so I'm not slouching. He can't stand slouchers.

He lifts his ball cap and runs a hand over his thinning dark hair, tucking it under the hat before he leans back into his chair.

"How's the new semester going for you? Are you keeping yourself busy, son?"

I think twice about answering honestly because in truth, I don't know what to say. Telling him the truth would only prove I'm struggling with the new routine and the lack of camaraderie I've always had in the past. I'd never admit to feeling like a failure. Not to Coach.

And I definitely can't mention anything about my love life and what's going on between me and Lottie.

So instead, I go with a vague response. "It's going, Coach. Grad school is..." I pause, trying to find the words to articulate how I'm feeling about it. "I like my classes."

Coach clears his throat with one of those noises he always makes that sound like a cross between a choke and a gurgle. "Hmm...good for you. Glad to hear it. So, what brings you by the field today?"

An awkward silence descends around us. My brain spins to explain the reason for my unannounced appearance. "Oh, you know, just popping by to check in with the guys, see how the team is gelling so far this season."

It's clear Coach doesn't believe me because his bushy eyebrows lift to the ceiling and then his eyes narrow in on me. Leaning forward, he stretches his forearms out in front of him and clasps his hands together. Then he points one finger at me.

"Your timing is serendipitous, Hendy. I was just racking my brain trying to figure out how I'm going to fill the unexpected open position Coach Peters just left me with."

"Huh? Where did Petey go?"

Coach Peters was my quarterback coach for the Bears and has been doing it for at least fifteen years or more. He's a symbol of consistency and dedication in this program, much like Coach Brewster.

Coach sighs. "This stays between us for now," he says with stern warning. Removing his ball cap again, he runs a hand over his hair, purses his lips, and shakes his head. "I just heard from his wife, Maggie. Petey had some tests done and they found cancer. I don't know the extent of it yet, but he'll be out effective immediately."

"Oh, shit."

"Yeah, oh shit is right. I was literally just about to call Human Resources to discuss next steps on finding a temporary replacement."

My fingers find the rubber band wrapped around my left wrist and I unconsciously snap it, feeling the slight burn into my skin. I've always worn it since I was in middle school. It helps me when I'm trying to concentrate or when I get anxious, a trick I learned from one of my former teachers.

"That might be tough," I offer unnecessarily. "First game is just a week away."

He snorts. "Tell me something I don't know. Which is why you showing up out of the blue is my answered prayer. You are the right person at the right time."

The rubber band slips from my fingers and snaps me

harder than I expect, stinging the flesh of my wrist. I rub at it and try to comprehend what Coach is saying.

"Um...what do you mean?"

He chuckles. "Henderson, you're the perfect person for this role. You know my coaching style. You know the playbook. You know all the staff and the majority of players. You have the leadership skills we need. You were made for this position, son. What do you say?"

This isn't what I expected to happen when I stopped by to see how things were going. I'm still confused as to what he's looking for from me. Is he asking me if I want a job on the coaching staff?

"What do I say about *what*?" I ask again, my brain clearly muddled like I've just been sacked out on the field.

"Did the summer leave you dense, Hendy?" He jokes with a laugh. "I'm offering you a temporary QB coach position, if you have the time and want a job. Of course, I'd need to run this by HR and have all the paperwork drawn up, but once we dot some i's and cross some t's. You could get started before our first game."

* * *

"Are you serious, bro?" Emmett asks, his voice pitched high incredulously over this news, his face filling the video chat screen on my phone. "Coach Brewster offered you a job, just like that?"

"Yeah, bro. On the spot, just like that." I snap my fingers. "Why is that so hard to fathom?"

EJ snickers, and I see him shrug just as he tries to maim my avatar on the video game we've been playing over the past hour. The girls, including my little sister Journey, are all out of the house tonight at some student volunteerism thing, and I have the place all to myself.

I never thought I'd live in a house full of women. But I have to admit, it sure smells a lot nicer here than it did when only football players occupied the place. And they're much better housemates because they clean up after themselves.

"It sounds like a perfect gig for you, dude. You can take Levitt under your wing and show him how it's done."

EJ's referring to Colson Levitt, a freshman and starting QB, who is a young cocky player with nothing but his high school stats to back it up. I like the kid well enough, but he has a lot to learn for sure. At least when I came on the team as a freshman, I had a year on the sidelines before the senior QB graduated, and I learned a ton from watching him play.

"Yeah, I suppose I can," I agree, clicking furiously on my controller. "It's just hard to wrap my head around the idea that I'll be coaching rather than out on the field playing."

It still amazes me that Coach offered me the job. I thought my football days were over and I'd never get near the field again after last year. If I take the job, it will make my schedule ridiculously busy, but it would keep my mind and body occupied and my focus on something other than classes and my sexy professor.

I haven't mentioned that part to anyone else, not even EJ or Killer. While they are my best friends, I don't feel comfortable sharing the details of what's going on between Lottie and me with them. Especially since it may be a nonissue. She plans on speaking to the dean tomorrow anyway, and that will be that. Over and done, and I'll need to move on.

A foreign pain jabs me in the heart as I consider the outcome.

EJ continues talking—mostly trash talking as he blows shit up on the screen—but I tune out.

All I can think about is not being around Lottie.

And I don't like it.

Not one fucking bit.

A loud explosion happens on the screen and EJ rejoices with a, "Take that, asshole!"

But I'm already on my phone tapping out a message to Lottie.

Me: I'm coming over. We need to talk. I'm having trouble with this assignment.

Chapter Nine

Charlotte

I stare at my phone.

Should I leave and just not be here when he rings my bell? He says he needs to talk, but nothing good can come of that. I wouldn't allow any of my other students to show up unannounced at my door.

He's not just any student, I think testily.

While my mind races with possibilities of what to do and how to handle this conundrum, I'm already in search of a cute outfit. I'm mad at myself for caving so easily. This absolutely can't happen again. In fact, I should put on my grungiest track pants and a crumpled-up T-shirt. There's no reason I need to look good for Joel.

My phone buzzes, and as if we somehow share a tele-pathic link, I see Poppy's name appear on my screen. How is it that my best friend always seems to sense when I need her most?

"I was just thinking of you," I state and toss the phone on the bed so I can start undressing.

"Oh? Have you gone to the dean yet?" she asks without preamble. I pause. Why is she asking that?

"Not yet, why?" I pull on a new off-the-shoulder jumper. The temperature here in the mountains has begun to drop and I feel as though I'm in England in the winter.

"Don't do it. I've put a lot of thought into this, and I think you should see where this goes with your hot student." I freeze again. This is a complete mindfuck. I can't have my bestie acting like the naughty devil on my shoulder, encouraging me to do something bad.

It would be a lie if I said I didn't want to be with Joel. But I can't do it. It's a no-win situation. Being with him means risking my career. Yet I've never felt an attraction so strong that I was willing to risk everything to be with a man. Will I miss out on the potential love of my life if I put an end to things with Joel?

"Sod off," I snipe miserably. "Seriously, Pops. It's wrong and we both know it. And you need to be the voice of reason for me."

She sighs and I know she's rolling her eyes, which only increases my irritation further.

"I'm serious. I can't keep doing this with him. My entire reputation is on the line here. No man is worth that," I explain through gritted teeth, even though I can't help but think of what I'll miss.

"But, Lots, what if he's the one? You don't want to let this go just because of some drama that won't even exist in a few more months, do you?" she prods in that persuasive manner of hers. "You've never been one to give up without a fight."

I take a deep breath and consider my next words carefully. "For the sake of argument, let's just say I decide to continue things with Joel and give this relationship a go. And then someone finds out about the circumstances in which we met last spring. It could ruin my whole academic career and reputation, and then what? I came here to get away from a situation that almost derailed my dreams and I'd be putting myself right back into one."

I think of how Oliver treated me when we were together. How he verbally abused me and put me down, nearly ruining my self-esteem. How he grabbed my arm during that last fight we had. How I almost fell apart after that. It nearly ended me and my pursuit of my education and career. I had to dig deep inside myself to muster the courage to leave and put myself first. And I did it. I got into the doctoral program in Boston, and I promised myself to never let a man get between me and my career again.

"Joel is not the man who shall not be named. This is different. You talked about this guy for months after meeting him last spring. You two had a connection then and clearly still do. I say, as your best friend, you should get over your worries and just go for it. Screw everything else. Just go for it."

The doorbell rings and my heart lurches with anticipation because on the other side of that door is Joel. I smooth my hair down and check myself in the mirror.

"Nice talk. Thanks, Pops. I have to go. I'll ring back later," I say in one breath, hanging up and walking to my front door. My head spins with each step.

What am I going to do? Even as I stand on this precipice of indecision, I am no closer to figuring it out.

When I open the door, I find him standing there, his head slightly bent at an angle, thumbs hooked in his jean pockets, casually leaning against the front porch railing. Looking like he belongs here, without a care in the world.

Of course, he looks hot enough to fuck with his messy hair and chiseled jaw. How is a woman supposed to stand firm and not cave when this man is in front of her? The universe is so unfair.

"May I come in?" he asks, lifting his flirtatious gaze to me. When I don't move and remain silent—I'm not even sure what to say—the corners of his mouth curve into a knowing grin.

He glides forward with that cocky confidence of his, sidestepping me as he enters the house, and I shut the door behind him. The minute I turn around, his body crowds mine against the door, his strong arms caging me in as he leans forward.

He inhales, breathing in the scent of me, and my own breath stops, my stomach flutters wildly.

"Mmm...you smell good, Professor," he murmurs, running the tip of his nose along my cheek before planting a gentle kiss on it. Then he takes a step back, offering me much-needed space to think straight, and makes a sweeping glance around my living room, as if he never got a good look the first time he was here.

I step away from the door and into the room, side-stepping Joel to take a seat on the sofa all while making myself a promise to keep my lustful behavior buried tonight. My stomach takes this moment to loudly protest with a hungry growl and I realize I haven't had dinner yet. Joel's eyebrows fly to the ceiling.

"Have you eaten? I was thinking of ordering some Chinese takeaway."

Joel moves to the smaller sofa across from me and sits down. "Sure. I could eat. Sounds good. Thanks."

I pull up the delivery app for the only Chinese restaurant in town, trying to stall this conversation and catch my breath. But I can't help watching out of the corner of my eye as Joel casually extends an arm along the back of the cushions ever so coolly, his legs opening into a V as he effortlessly props one foot over a knee. The move has his T-shirt tightening to outline the rolling hills of his abdominals underneath, and the denim of his jeans stretches oh-so-perfectly over his muscular thighs, outlining what I know is a very large package.

It's easy to see why so many women on campus—and probably men too—are obsessed with him. He's sexy when he's not even trying.

I give myself a mental shake. Stop this madness immediately.

Taking a spot on the chair across from the couch, I punch in my order and then hand the phone over to him. He takes it from me, looks at it and then sets it down next to him. Then he pulls out his own phone and dials a number that must be in his contacts.

"Yo, Big Mike. It's Hendy. I need to place an order to go. Yep. Awesome." I give him an incredulous look. Didn't I have this handled?

Hendy rattles off a list of food that could probably feed an entire football team, including the items on my list.

"Uh-huh. Yep. Thanks. See you in fifteen."

"What was that all about?" I ask, completely perplexed by what just transpired.

Hendy gives me a lopsided grin. "I know the owner and his son. Mike and I had a class together when he was a senior and I was a sophomore. He needed some help getting football tickets for his dad's business partner and I hooked them up. Since then, I've been a VIP." He pauses and shrugs. "Perks of being a football player in a college town. What can I say?"

Of course he's friends with the owner. Why wouldn't he be? Hendy is known in these parts by everyone.

If CFU had a mayor, it'd be Hendy.

Joel moves and stretches, his T-shirt lifting a fraction of an inch to display those ridiculous abs, and I look away. Gah. I can't even trust myself to look at him, much less be near him.

Which brings us back to the reason why he's here tonight.

"You said you wanted to talk to me, and here you are. So go ahead. While we wait for dinner, say what you need to say." I hope to sound convincing, even though my hands shake with nerves and there's a slight tremor in my voice. I slip my hands under my butt and draw my heels up on the couch cushion.

He purses his lips in consideration and finally nods. "Okay...why did you come to the US?"

"What? That's a random question and not what I thought we'd be discussing."

He laughs and shrugs. "Just want to get to know you better."

I throw out my hand for him to stop. "Nuh-uh. There is no need for that because after tonight, this ends."

"Come on...indulge me a little," he says in a crestfallen voice. "I'll tell you anything you want to know about me. Open book."

"Joel," I say, a pleading look in my eyes. "We can't. You're my student."

He lifts his brows. "Technically, we're now colleagues. And friends."

Friends? Does he mean with benefits?

Is there a world where Joel and I could exist as friends? I'm not so sure.

"What? How is that, exactly?" I reply, my voice raising an octave. Does that mean he's dropping out and not finishing his master's program? If so, that definitely changes things.

"I got a job offer with the university today," he says. As if that's not a big deal.

This has taken a weird turn. "Doing what?"

"Coaching football."

"American football or 'real' football?" I jest, unable to help myself.

Joel barks out a laugh, wagging his finger at me. "I'm not talking soccer. Good one, though."

"What does that mean for your grad program?"

"Nothing really, except I think I'll be very busy this semester." He looks down at the time on his phone. "I'd rather be busy than bored though, you know? It'll keep my thoughts off of other things I can't have." He gazes intently at me, and I not only hear but see his innuendo.

Joel stands suddenly and reaches for my hand to help me up. "We should go pick up that food. And then maybe we can catch one of your *real* football games on TV?"

I pause at the threshold, my hand stuck on the doorknob, suddenly nervous about people seeing us together. Before I can express this concern, Hendy leans forward, his large palm gently covering my hand, which trembles under his touch.

"Don't worry. If anyone asks, I'll just say I'm your new research assistant and we are working on a paper," he assures me, his breath hot against my ear. "Trust me. I'll be good."

Good...but something inside me wants him to be bad.

* * *

We pick up our takeaway and walk back toward my house. As we turn the corner and cross to the other side of the street, Joel positions himself between me and the road. That small gesture of chivalry makes me feel safe, as if Hendy would fight off an entire army to protect me.

"The game tonight is Tottenham versus Chelsea. It started an hour ago, but I'm recording it," I explain.

"Ahh...so I'll get to see the 'real' game of football. I can't wait." He bumps me with his hip, and I giggle like a schoolgirl.

"You have much to learn. They're Premier League football teams."

With the game turned on, we grab spots on my couch, setting our food and drinks between us. We eat and watch in comfortable silence for a few minutes until the ref makes a terrible call.

"Oh, come on!" I yell. "That was offsides!"

"I don't think so. Watch the replay. I'm pretty sure it was the right call," Hendy says.

I glare at him and then watch the replay. And bloody hell, he's right. Dammit, this is supposed to be my game.

"How do you know the rules of football?" I ask testily, crossing my arms over my chest. His eyes drop to my breasts and I swat his shoulder. "Eyes up here, Henderson."

He chuckles and shrugs. "I mean, I've played every FIFA PlayStation game since I was like ten. Not too hard to catch on."

I roll my eyes. "Of course you have."

He smirks. God damn him and those lips. My body heats up at the memory of what those lips can do to me.

I stuff another bite of Kung Pao Chicken into my mouth and avert my gaze from his mouth.

For the next two hours, we watch the match and argue over the virtues of both types of football. By the end of the match, we're both shouting at the refs and when my favorite player scores in the last minute of the match, Hendy gives me a hug, lifting me off my feet and swinging me around in celebration.

It scares me how good it feels in his arms, so when he sets me down, I quickly dash into the kitchen.

"I'm still hungry," I mutter, quickly grabbing the half-eaten jar of Nutella and smearing it on a slice of bread. "You?"

"Whatcha got for dessert?"

When I come back to the living room licking my lips, Joel stares at me as if he wants a taste of me.

"What's that?"

"Only the most delicious thing ever," I state, taking another unladylike bite. "Nutella sandwich."

He makes a gagging nose and wrinkles his nose.

"Don't yuck my yum," I say defensively. "Who doesn't like Nutella?"

"Me."

"That's one strike," I tease, popping the last bite into my mouth.

He leans over the tray of empty containers between us, his voice as seductive as ever. "What happens if I get three strikes?"

"I don't actually know," I answer truthfully because I really don't know what we're doing right now.

Are we flirting? Is this some kind of foreplay between us?

In the end, Joel forgoes dessert, and we share a little about each other's families and our backgrounds. He tells me about his younger sister attending CFU this year, his time with the football team, and his nerves about starting the coaching position.

None of it has solved our growing problem and the attraction between us that can't be squelched.

By the time my eyelids begin to grow heavy and I curl up against Hendy's side on the loveseat, I've reassured myself that Joel and I can find a way to just be friends.

"I'm exhausted," I mutter, finally letting my eyelids close.

"Come on, Professor. Let's get you to bed." His voice seems far away, and I feel weightless and safe when he picks me up and carries me down the hallway.

The last thing I remember as I drift off to sleep is wishing this man could be lying asleep next to me.

Chapter Ten

H endy

I remained at Lottie's house for another thirty minutes before I reluctantly left last night. The rise and fall of her chest with each soft breath had me mesmerized as I sat at the edge of her bed and watched her sleep. I traced the reddish-gold locks of her hair that fanned out over her pillow, brushing away loose strands off her forehead.

Never before had I ever cared enough about a woman to be content just watching her sleep. In the past, if I were in bed with a woman, I'd have fucked her hard and then high-tailed it out of there.

But my feelings for Lottie are different and go way beyond that need. Don't get me wrong. I was dying to get naked, climb into her bed, and touch every inch of her until we were breathless and sated. But I resisted, respecting the boundaries she'd set, and left when the urge to lay down beside her became too strong.

It still took every ounce of my willpower to walk out that door.

But I did.

The idea that we can try to tamp down our feelings and sexual attraction to be friends is ridiculous. I know it. She knows it. But I understand her reasons for setting those limits for the sake of her career.

I get it. I respect her for it. But it doesn't mean I have to like it.

Now that I have this position on the team, maybe it wouldn't be too hard to table the graduate degree for a while and pursue a relationship with Lottie. We could date like any other two consenting adults and school colleagues. No conflict of interest at all.

I like who I am when I'm with her. Like I'm the man I'm meant to become.

Fuck, I need to stop all this waxing poetic and get a grip.

There's laughter coming from inside the kitchen as I enter the front of our house and some pop music is playing on Spotify in the living room, but nobody is in here. The entire vibe in the house is vastly different than it was last year. That's when this was considered the football house and there would always be a bunch of guys hanging out playing video games, eating pizza, and drinking beer.

Now things are...girly as fuck. It's not a bad thing, just different.

Turning the corner into the kitchen, I see Kelsie and Grace standing side-by-side at the counter, making something that smells delicious, and Lucy at the sink.

"Hey, what's cooking, ladies?"

Lucy whips around with a spatula in her hand. "We're

making a birthday cake for your sister's birthday party tomorrow."

My eyes grow wide in alarm, and I look down at the date of September twenty-eight on my watch. Oh shit. I completely spaced on that. Journey is turning nineteen tomorrow.

I groan. "Aww, fuck. I forgot and didn't get her anything."

Kelsie hoots out in an exasperated huff. "Just get her a box of condoms. She'll need them."

"What the fuck, Kels?" I choke out the question with a cough. "Why would you say that about my little sister?"

I look at Grace, whose brows reach the ceiling, and Kelsie swings around with a bowl full of chocolate cake batter. She tilts her head to the side and gives me a look like I'm the biggest idiot alive.

"Dude, she's not nine. And considering she is going out on a date this weekend with the captain of the hockey team, she is going to need some protection."

I suddenly feel dizzy and see red. "The fuck she is! Why the hell is she going out with Ben Hoff-steader?"

Kelsie pours the batter into a prepared cake pan as Grace assists by swiping a second spatula around the bowl to get it cleaned out and then swipes her finger over the rim of the bowl.

Gracie licks her finger while Kelsie replies, stealing the chocolate covered spatula back from Grace. "Because I introduced them earlier this week," Kelsie says with a casual shrug. "Ben's a nice guy, and he'd mentioned being interested in Journey."

I dip my finger into the bowl of remaining batter and slide it over my tongue, allowing myself a second to calm my raging thoughts before I go caveman big brother on Kelsie's ass.

"Wasn't he the guy you dated before Hayes? Why would you give my little sister sloppy seconds?"

Kelsie throws a punch at my shoulder, but I use my quick reflexes to dodge away and she misses. However, she does manage to get a splatter of chocolate over my shirt from the spatula in her hand, which I wipe away on a dish towel.

Kelsie sets the empty bowl in the sink, Gracie wisely staying out of this discussion as she begins washing and drying the dirty dishes. Kels leans her back against the counter, fingers wrapped along the counter's edge.

"Bro, you're one to talk about sloppy seconds," she argues and I almost grimace. She has a point.

I cringe, thinking back to what a total dick I was a few years ago, after Lucy and Emmett broke up while on our ski vacation. Like a douche canoe of a friend, I immediately jumped in and tried to win her over. Those were the days I was all about myself.

Thankfully, that never came to fruition, and they got together like destiny planned. I'm also glad both EJ and Lucy forgave me for being such a tool and we're all still close friends. It could have easily gone the other direction.

"Anyway," Kelsie continues, "Ben and I never really dated because I was in love with a hot football kicker."

As if right on cue, Hayes walks into the kitchen carrying a backpack slung over his shoulder and heads straight to Kelsie, cupping her face in his hands and kissing her senseless.

It has Kels moaning with pleasure. The rest of us just groan at their pathetic PDA.

When he finally releases her, Mac says, "Hey baby.

Mmm...you taste *bonne.*" He swipes his tongue over her lips again and she sighs, eyelashes fluttering.

"Jesus Christ, get a room, you two."

Gracie giggles and finally chimes in. "I think it's hot when a man shows his woman just how much he missed her. Killian's really good with that part, too."

A swash of pink colors her cheekbones and I roll my eyes at my friends, who are all lovesick humans.

But a part of me is jealous that they all can so openly show their affections with each other. I want to be able to do that with Lottie.

"So, why was I the topic of conversation?" Hayes moves to the table, where he pulls out a chair and plunks down, setting his bag on the floor next to his feet.

"We weren't, exactly," I comment, opening the fridge to extract two beer bottles. I hand one to Hayes and sit down at the table next to him. "My sister is going out with a hockey player, and I don't approve."

Mac chuckles. "Better he goes out with your sister than the girl I love."

His eyes search out Kelsie who blows him a kiss. "It was never going to be the hockey player for me, baby. It was only ever you."

I drop my forehead to the table with a thunk. "Do you guys have to be so fucking sappy? It's disgusting."

Kelsie steps up next to my chair and ruffles my hair with her now dry hands. "Aww...what got you into such a pissy mood tonight? Are you not getting any hot loving these days, QB?"

No. Not anymore.

I snort. "As if."

My head swings toward the back door as it flies open and Journey enters the conversation. She brings with her the bluest cornflower-blue eyes and the brightest white-toothed smile of anyone I know.

"Please don't tell me you're talking about my brother's sex life. I feel like we should all get tested regularly for STIs just for living under the same roof as him."

I stare, affronted at my baby sister's audacity. She appears to me now as a college-aged woman, not the little girl in braces from a few years ago. When did she grow up?

"I will let that one pass, only because I'm a nice guy. And I want to know about this date with you and Ben."

Journey opens the fridge to pull out a juice box, and I'm hit with an image of her at age six. When she turns back around, I get a closer look at the clothes she's wearing. Or not wearing, it seems. She has on a cropped T-shirt that exposes her midriff and a pair of workout shorts.

I'm about to say something to the effect of *what the fuck are you wearing* when Grace pipes in with a loud exclamation. "That's weird...come to think of it, I haven't seen one girl in this house with Hendy this fall. Did you turn into a monk, bro?"

No. Just fucking my professor on the DL.

I flip her off and she laughs that light, airy laugh of hers.

"Yeah, what's up with that? Very unlike you," Kelsie says, taking a seat next to me and fixing me with her intense green-eyed stare. "You hiding something we don't know about?"

Shit, man. Is Kels a mind reader?

I blanch and disconnect my gaze from hers, focusing my attention on my beer bottle.

"No. Of course not. Don't be dumb." Even to my own ears, my voice sounds overly exaggerated and fake.

With the reflexes of a lioness in waiting, Kelsie's hand darts out and she lifts my chin so our eyes meet.

"Are you fucking that new British professor on campus?"

Instead of denying it, the words just tumble out of my mouth, and I give it all up to my witchy friend. I'd never make a good spy.

"How did you know?"

Kelsie slams her palm on the table. "Boom! I fucking knew it!"

She leaps out of her chair and points her index finger at me and everyone else stares at me in complete silence, as if I've completely lost my mind.

"I noticed you two walking across campus on my way to the grocery store earlier. Those heart-eyes you were giving her were a dead giveaway! Now, spill the tea, dude. Give us all the details of how she stole your heart."

For a moment, I sit there completely frazzled, incredulous that she could read me so well. But then I cave and start telling them about how Lottie and I originally met, providing them with the timeline and what went down earlier this semester.

When I finish sharing all the deets and where things left off with Lottie tonight, everyone is speechless.

Kelsie is the first one to speak, her eyes wide with a strange fascination. "OMG. Our boy is in love."

"Yeah, but it's a doomed love story," Journey pipes in sadly. "Lottie shut it down."

After a few minutes, Grace stands up and moves behind my chair, placing her hands on top of my shoulders. She clears her throat, and says in an even-keeled voice, "Not to fear, QB. I know exactly what you need to do to win her over."

Chapter Eleven

Charlotte

"If you haven't sent me your paper outlines yet, please do so by Sunday night," I say, glancing around the room full of students. *My* students, I think proudly.

A young woman in the front of the classroom raises her hand.

"Yes, Daniella?" I keep my gaze firmly on her and avoid looking at Hendy in the same row a few seats to her right.

"I thought the syllabus said they were due Friday." She frowns as her fingers click across her keyboard, clearly checking the original due date.

"They were, but you're in luck because I'll be away this weekend," I explain, shoving my laptop into my bag. "So you'll have extra time to complete the assignment."

"Sweet," a male student exclaims loudly from the back of the room. Some other students snicker.

I give him a look that says, *Keep it up and it'll be due today*.

"Sorry, Professor. It's just good news," he mumbles.

"Alright, then. I'll see you all next week and will look for your completed work in my inbox Sunday night."

The students begin to leave as I pack up the rest of my bag and head out the room. Bypassing my office, which I'd already locked up, I head downstairs to the building exit. When I step outside, I have to shield my eyes from the bright sunshine that streams across my face. It solidifies the decision I made earlier today to get away this weekend and go hiking up in the mountains. I need time to get away and clear my head and to figure out what I'm going to do about Joel.

I stop in the middle of the quad and close my eyes for a moment to enjoy the warmth. I didn't know this kind of thing in England between the clouds and rain of the fall. Suddenly a large shadow blocks the sun's rays and the warmth is lost.

"Where are you going this weekend, Professor?"

My eyes fly open and squint up at Joel, who stands in front of me with a scowl across his face. Clearly, he's displeased. "Away..." I offer vaguely, not wanting to start this conversation out in the open, as I stare up at his handsome features.

It's so difficult not to want to kiss him. I miss the feel of his lips on me. I miss the slide of my fingers over his skin.

I just miss him in the way one misses a lover.

He raises an eyebrow, awaiting a better response.

"Fine," I acquiesce. "If you must know, I'm going hiking."

"Alone? Where?" Is that concern in his questions? Or is he looking to invite himself along?

I give him a pointed look. He doesn't budge, obviously intent on getting this information from me.

I'm suddenly tired of resisting him. It's the reason I want to get away this weekend—so I can clear my head and my heart of this mess. I really need to discuss it with the dean and let go of the guilt I carry every day that I lie about my relationship with Joel. Taking in a deep breath, I rest my butt against the wood of a table in the quad.

"The Clearview Falls ski resort. My cousin's home is available, and I want some time alone...in nature." It's the truth.

As much as we were able to hang out the other night and keep our hands off each other, it nearly killed me not to touch him. When he picked me up and carried me into my bedroom, I wanted so badly to open my eyes and tell him to stay. But I didn't for obvious reasons. And now, I'm left in this purgatory of wanting something I can't have.

Why must he be my student?

The good thing is that we're already scheduled for midterms next week and after that, there are only six weeks left before the end of the semester. And then I'll be grading twenty research papers before Christmas break. The task is daunting but fills me with a serene sense of accomplishment. This position is everything I'd ever hoped for, and I love working for this university.

"Hmmm. Well, that changes things," he mutters, turning around to leave. "I gotta go. Enjoy your weekend."

"Wait, what?" I ask, confused. "What changes things?"

Without another word, he leaves with a wave over his shoulder, and I watch as he walks toward the student center and then disappears from sight.

A million thoughts burst inside my mind like fireworks.

Should I have asked him to come with me? Should I have restated the boundary I set the other night?

I still haven't spoken to the dean yet because we aren't currently doing anything unethical and haven't crossed any lines, even if my thoughts of Joel are completely inappropriate.

The fact remains: Will I give Joel a chance after the semester is over?

As I walk back home, I contemplate that last question. Honestly, I don't know yet.

* * *

Wildflowers of purple, white, and red paint the scenery from where I sit overlooking the valley below. It looks a lot different than it did last March. Although snow still covers the mountain peaks, nature is still harboring the last wisps of fall down here. The gold and yellow leaves of the cottonwoods and aspens are a beautiful contrast to the green of the pines. A gentle breeze blows across my face, and I breathe in the fresh air and lean back on the rock, staring up at the sky.

A restorative peace settles in my belly.

My life has never been simple, by any means. Privileged, maybe, but not easy when you grow up with a demanding father like mine. And right now, although I'm on my own, my life is a complex weave of uncertainty.

My classes are going well, and I've made a few faculty friends. I love the teaching aspect of my role but the amount of review and grading that has to be done is enormous. I've burnt the midnight oil prepping for my courses the next day or reading through outlines and student papers, not to mention the work I've put into my research paper. Making a good impression with my colleagues and seeing my students excel in the learning environment is rewarding and fulfilling.

Would I even have time for a relationship with Joel if the opportunity presented itself? I'd be heartbroken if I let him go and didn't try to make something work, though, because he's the kind of man I could see myself with forever.

My phone buzzes in my pocket and startles me out of my silent retreat. Of course it's Poppy calling to check up on me.

"How's the hike going, Lots? You haven't fallen off a cliff, have you? Will I need to send medical aid?"

I lean my head over a bit to see the drop below and rear back. It's definitely a long way down.

"Nope. No aid required," I add confidently, drawing a circle with my finger over the boulder's smooth surface.

"Not even the aid of your sexy student?" she asks devilishly.

I fight a smile, imagining Joel sitting next to me on this mountain top.

"Truthfully, I was just thinking about that...situation."

"Great, then go do it—or him."

"We've been over this, Pops. You know it's complicated. Joel is great—not to mention young." I groan. "It's maybe the right man at the wrong time. Even if he weren't my student, I don't know if I'm ready to give a relationship a go." And for reasons I can't explain or maybe don't want to admit, my eyes well with tears.

A loud peel of laughter howls through the phone line. So loud, in fact, I have to pull the phone from my ear, and I think I get an evil glare from a bird up in the tree above me.

"For the love of God, Lottie! The man is not Oliver. He

won't hurt you. Everything you've told me about this chap has *me* wanting to marry the goddamn bloke!" she insists. "If you could hear what I hear in your voice when you talk about him, it's very revealing. I know he's perfect for you. You just won't admit it."

For once, she sounds exasperated.

I am, too.

"It's scary," I admit, and grab my water bottle to wet my parched throat.

"I know it is. But you're brave, lovey. Hell, you're the bravest woman I know. You moved halfway around the world to escape your shitty ex. You got yourself into one of the hardest academic programs for your field. And then you up and moved across that continent to start a career. You did all of that. On. Your. Own," she emphasizes, and I grin.

"Bravery won't help my ethical dilemma, though, will it?" I point out, grabbing my hiking gear and heading back down the trail.

"It will. You just have to work around it or fix it," she suggests.

"How?"

She heaves a sigh. "I don't know. You're smart. Figure it out. Talk to him and make a plan to wait it out, then shag him after he turns in his final paper."

I pause at her last statement. "Hmm...I suppose I could do that. Or after I grade it."

It's still too risky. There's still the possibility that students or faculty will find out and then think we've had an affair the entire semester and I played favorites with him.

"What if I wait and he graduates but gets a job and moves away? Then what?" I ask, looking down at the bumpy path to avoid any accidental falls.

"Cross that bridge in another six months. You spend far

too much time thinking about the future. Just live in the moment, Lots."

She's not wrong. I do spend too much time worrying about things that are eons away.

"I'll consider it," I finally say so she'll let this go. I know she wants what's best for me, but I still need to think things over.

"That's my girl. Now, shall I tell you about my hot man and his friend I shagged last night?"

I choke and nearly trip over my feet.

"Pops, I'm trying to pay attention to the trail! Jesus Christ, you can't spring that on me when I'm hiking."

She doesn't seem to care and begins telling me about how she met the two men in a bar and their hot hookup that went on all night.

Sometimes I wish I could be more like Poppy. She's fearless when it comes to sex and men.

After she finishes, I think I need a drink.

"Talk later?"

"Of course. But I'm serious, don't give up on this one, Lots. If he makes you happy, don't lose out on that. You deserve to be happy."

"Thanks, Pops. I miss you," I state sadly.

"You're welcome. And I miss you too. Kisses," she says, and the line goes dead.

I slide my phone back into my pocket and wonder what I would do without her.

She's not wrong. I don't give myself enough credit and I shouldn't push away my chance at happiness.

Maybe there is a way to make this work and I should give us a chance.

Chapter Twelve

H^{endy}

The soft knock on my door has my eyes flying open and my head popping up from the book it's currently planted in.

"Yeah?" I ask, my voice sounding gravely from sleep. I rub my cheek where it was smashed against the textbook and glance down at the time on my phone. It reads 9:45 p.m. I must've fallen asleep over an hour ago.

The door creaks open and Grace's face comes into view as she pushes through into my bedroom.

"How's it going in here?" she asks, peering around the mess. I comb the hair back from my eyes. "I thought you could use a study break snack."

My stomach rumbles when she steps in and hands a plate of food out at me, topped with a sandwich, chips and a very large slice of cake leftover from Journey's birthday party.

Grace walks over to my desk and sets the plate down on a stack of books.

"To what do I owe this unexpected pleasure?" I grab for the sandwich and take a huge bite, my mouth filling with the sweet and tangy flavor of pastrami and mustard. My favorite.

She plops down on the study chair, folds her legs into a pretzel, and tucks her feet underneath her butt. Her dark hair is damp from a recent shower and she has on her cat pajamas and glasses. She gives me a serious look.

"How are you coming with your plans to win over your professor?"

I let my eyes drift back to my open laptop, now dark because it shut down while I was sleeping. I bring it back to life with a touch of the track pad. The screen lights up and the words I'd written on the page reappear.

"It's good. I think I'm almost done with the first draft. Tomorrow, I plan to edit it and then I have the meeting with the dean to submit it."

"Nice going, Hendy." Gracie lifts her palm toward me and I give her a high five. "I'll be honest, I didn't think you had it in you to pull this off."

I scoff. "Come on now...I'm way more brilliant than the oaf you call your boyfriend."

She squeaks incredulously and punches me in the arm. "Hey! Don't be disparaging of my man. Killian is smart where it counts."

I snort out in laughter and roll my eyes. "How is farm boy these days anyway? We haven't had a chance to talk lately because of our schedules."

A dreamy expression appears on her face and she smiles wistfully. My God, this girl has it bad for my friend. It's kind of cute. She and Killer are complete opposites. Grace is a sweet and highly intelligent STEM student, and Killian is a big lug of a man who works with animals and crops on his family's farm in Iowa.

"Killian's good. He's been super busy getting that farm updated to all the new standards, but they've had a great harvest this fall so far. He's planning on coming for a visit over Halloween weekend."

I look at the calendar and can't believe how fast the time has gone. Since starting my new role on the football team staff, I've barely managed to get time to sleep. Between attending classes, coaching, and getting ahead on this brilliant plan of Grace's to win over Lottie, I'm working my fucking ass off each and every day. It's exhausting. But I'm following the advice of Grace and working on my plan to have Lottie in my life as someone other than my professor. As someone I'd like to call my girlfriend.

"That's cool. Maybe by then, if she'll have me, I can take this public, and she can come to our Halloween party."

Gracie literally bounces in her seat and claps her hands together. "Oh my God, that would be so awesome. When's your meeting scheduled?"

Now it's me who wears a dopey big heart-eyes expression on my face as I think about how great it would be if my plan works out. I know where Professor Butler stands on the whole dating a student issue. Which is why this plan we've come up with—the one that has me breaking my back to finish my coursework—should move things in the right direction.

"It's Monday, when Lottie returns from her hiking trip."

Grace stands up from her seat and ruffles my hair with her hand before she heads to the door.

"I hope you can get some rest between now and then. You'll need it."

"Why's that?" I ask.

She glances over her shoulder with a saucy wink. "Obvs because of the massive amount of make-up sex you'll be having."

My friend is a smart woman. I like the sound of that.

* * *

I sit across the deep-grained dark mahogany desk from Dean Becker, who leans back casually in his leather chair, and chat amiably with him about football while we wait for Lottie to arrive.

"You know, Hendy, I'm very impressed with what you've accomplished in such a short time. We are lucky to have a young man who has this much passion for achieving his goals."

It's funny. I used to be immune to those in authority roles doing what I thought was blowing smoke up my ass. I used to bring this university money with my starring role as QB One, after all. But now I'm just a normal guy on campus, even though I'm now part of the coaching staff and I now see it for the compliment that it's meant to be.

I'd called and requested this meeting with the dean so I could put all my cards on the table, so to speak. I care about Lottie and don't want to do anything to damage her reputation and career as an instructor at this educational institution. I'd rather take the hit on my own and keep her out of the fray until the time I can make my public grand gesture.

"Thanks, Dean." I clear my throat. "The past four plus years at CFU have been the best of my life, and I've learned a lot about myself and who I want to be. Especially this semester in Professor Butler's course. She's taught me..."

How to love. But I can't say that.

I rub the back of my neck, hoping he doesn't see through me and the reason I'm here.

"Professor Butler has taught me to pursue the things I want most in life and how to work hard to get them."

Dean nods, his expression indecipherable. His brows narrow, as if he's trying to read between the lines.

Folding his hands on his lap, he smiles tightly. "That's good to hear. As you know, Professor Butler is new to our school this year and is in her probationary period. She is being evaluated on academic course assessments, peer reviews, and of course, student evaluations."

Just then, there's a knock, and the dean's eyes divert from me to the door behind me. "Come in, please."

I remain composed, but the moment I turn my head to look at her, I lose my breath. Lottie walks in, her green eyes holding a bright smile for the dean, and then she literally jerks back and her smile diminishes when her gaze lands on me.

"Oh, excuse me. I thought we were meeting, sir," she says in apology, confusion etched across her beautiful face.

Dean gestures with a hand toward the chair next to mine. "Yes, please sit, Professor Butler. Mr. Henderson is the one who requested that we all meet together. I apologize I didn't make that clear in my meeting invite to you."

With one quick look, I can read the burning question on Lottie's mind: *What the hell are you doing?*

"Hello, Professor," I say in my most charming and unas-suming voice. "Thanks for joining us today. You probably didn't expect to see me in the dean's office."

She moves gracefully toward the chair, her fragrant scent wafting in the space between us, and I have to grab hold of the chair arms to steady myself. *Do not fuck this up,* I remind myself.

Once settled, she crosses one leg over the other and peers at me.

"What can we do for you, Mr. Henderson?"

Oh fuck. What can't she do for me?

She can turn me on. Turn me out. And turn me into a sappy, lovesick puppy.

But I keep those thoughts out of my head and off my face. That's step two of my plan. First, I need to get through Step One.

I lay my palm flat on the folder in my lap. In it is everything I need to move forward with my plan.

Operation: Make Lottie my Girlfriend.

"As you may or may not know, Professor, I recently accepted a job on the football team's coaching staff."

Lottie quirks an eyebrow. "Yes, I may have heard something about that. Congratulations, Mr. Henderson."

The corner of my mouth curves in a smile. "Thank you. *American football,* of course."

Her eyes twinkle at our inside joke.

I continue. "After much consideration, I've decided the best way to manage my limited time and to give my team the focus it deserves is for me to complete your course early. I have come prepared to submit my final paper to you in advance of the semester deadline."

"Very admirable, Mr. Henderson," Dean Becker interjects, pride in his voice. As if I'm doing *him* a favor. He glances at Lottie and leans forward. "Do you have any objections with his early submission, Professor Butler?"

I hand over the file folder that contains all the coursework from the syllabus and my final paper that I've worked on night and day over the weekend. When our fingers touch, a current of electricity runs up my arm.

When she accepts the folder, I notice a slight tremble of her hands. She opens it up, flipping through the printed-out assignments and paper.

"I printed it out for you, but I've also uploaded it all in the student portal for your review."

"Well, this is highly unusual..." she says cautiously.

"But I'm sure we can make the exception for Hendy, don't you?" The dean has stated it in the form of a question, but with an eyebrow raised. Lottie squirms in her chair uncomfortably.

I jump in, not wanting Lottie to feel bulldozed by any of this. I want her to see this as a good thing for both of us.

"Professor, I have learned so much while in your class. You're a wonderful instructor and you've made learning about marketing very interesting. I'd remain in your class if I could." I catch her gaze, my eyes blazing with meaning. I want her to know I'm doing this for her. Because I love her. "I just thought this would be a win-win and help me in my current *situation*."

I let the words dangle between us. She knows what situation I'm referring to. The situation of the two of us being in a relationship, exploring what's already started to grow between us.

The dean, however, thinks this is all about my new coaching position. He just smiles, like he's proud of my efficiency.

Lottie chews on her bottom lip, glancing down at the papers, then to me, and finally to the dean.

"I'll review everything this evening and let you know

tomorrow if anything has been missed. Assuming it's all in order, I'll submit your final grade before the fall break."

"Thank you for your time and consideration, Professor," I say, my eyes pleading with Lottie to understand why I've asked this of her, begging her to see that I've done this for us both.

It's my Hail Mary pass.

Let's hope it's enough to score and win the game.

* * *

Two Weeks Later

The grade popped up in my email inbox earlier this morning before I left for the morning practice. I waited to open it up and read it now as I walk across campus toward the field house.

Lottie gave me a B+.

I choke out a laugh loud enough to garner questionable looks from a few students around me in the quad. Although, they're the ones who should get the weird looks since they're all dressed up as alien creatures.

That's right. I nearly forgot that today is Halloween and the girls are throwing a Halloween party at our house.

It'll be great to see EJ and Killer, who are both back in town for a long overdue weekend visit. They even have tickets to tomorrow's Bears football game.

But it will be even better if I can convince Lottie to be my date to the party.

I veer course and turn in the other direction, toward Cameron Hall and Professor Butler's classroom.

Class begins in about ten minutes, so I have to book it if I want to get to her before she starts her seminar. The one I was a student in until two weeks ago.

My heart rate has sped up as I enter the building, rush-climb the stairs, and take a sharp left down the corridor. The doors to the room are open and there's a handful of students milling around, but I barely notice them. I have one goal in mind and she's at the front.

Lottie is next to the podium speaking with a classmate who always had a ton of questions during every session. She doesn't see my approach until I am standing behind the other woman, who is yammering on about the European markets and her trip to Greece.

Lottie's eyes grow wide and her forehead creases when she notices me. I give her my most charming smile.

The girl turns her head to see I'm standing behind her and seems to take the hint when I give her that look that says, *wrap it up, lady.*

"Oh, excuse me, Hendy. I was just asking Professor Butler a question. She's all yours."

I snicker at this because she has no idea how close to the truth that is. Or will be, I hope. "Thanks. I appreciate it."

When the woman moves out of earshot, I step in close. It catches Lottie by surprise, and she wobbles backward, but I catch her by the shoulders. Her eyes drift in alarm past my shoulder to the other students, and I shake my head.

"Let them see this."

And then I frame her face in my hands and seal my mouth over hers, tasting her warmth. The kiss is deep as my tongue makes a wet sweep inside. Sparks race through my blood with an electric excitement I haven't felt in weeks.

The feeling is short-lived, though, when a loud wolf whistle from the crowd carries down to where we stand, interrupting our kiss. Lottie jerks back, a palm pressed against my chest, and a surprised gasp is expelled from the lips I just tasted.

"What do you think you're doing?"

I tilt my head to the side. "It's not obvious?"

She stammers a few words in gibberish, shaking her head.

Then I take her hand in mine, pulling her to my side before I wrap an arm around her waist and tug her into me.

Addressing the class, which is now full of curious stares and censoring glances, I make my plan a reality.

"Many of you know me," I begin, and there's some applause and shouts across the room. "You know me as the Bears' QB. You know me as the guy on campus with a bad reputation when it comes to dating." More long whistles and a lot of snickers.

I take Lottie's hand and bring it to my heart, my hand covering hers.

"What you may not know is that I've fallen in love. I've never loved a woman before Lottie. Er, Charlotte," I correct. "I'm a man who has made a lot of mistakes in my past, but meeting Lottie has changed me. She's taught me valuable lessons about myself and that when it comes to love, it's better to give than receive. And right now, all I want to do is give everything I am to be with the woman I love."

Thunderous cheers and applause erupt throughout the room, but it's all drowned out by the crushing drum of my heartbeat in my ears.

Lottie stands there shell-shocked. I turn her so she's facing me and join both our hands together at our chests.

"Lottie, I love you. I've missed you and want to be with you. I want to make this official because now the rules have changed. The only question is whether you'll have me?"

I stare into her bright green eyes that now sparkle with unshed tears. She licks her bottom lip. "Will you be my girlfriend, Lottie?"

"I...I...oh, bugger. I can't believe you pulled a *Jerry Maquire* on me."

"What's that?"

She rolls her eyes. "Never mind. It's not important."

"But you are important to me. Will you say yes?"

"Yes, Joel," she gives me a watery smile that has my stomach doing a touchdown dance. "My answer is yes."

Epilogue

Charlotte

I look at myself in the mirror. I'm wearing a sexy nurse costume, which is apparently supposed to match Joel's doctor's costume. I feel a little silly, but he assured me that everyone would be dressed up for the party.

My cheeks turn pink as I remember how he kissed me in front of my class. I don't know what it was about that kiss, but it changed something in me. It was like a veil had been lifted and I saw the world clearly for the first time.

I grab my house key and stick it in the world's smallest pocket in the front of my outfit. The walk to Joel's only takes five minutes, but I quickly regret not bringing a coat. By the time I knock on the door and he answers, I'm shivering.

"Hey, sexy nurse. Are you cold? Get your cute ass in

here," he demands, yanking me inside and against him, warming my body instantly with his. Somehow, just the feel of his arms around me warms me and relaxes me. This is where I'm meant to be right now.

"I forgot a coat," I manage through the chatter of my teeth. "You *f-feel s-so g-good.*" I really underestimated how cold it gets up here in the mountains in October.

I press my body closer to him, partly for the heat and partly because I love the hard lines of muscles on his torso. His hands run lines up and down my back and after a minute, I feel myself thawing.

"Come on, let's get you a drink. It'll warm you up," he insists before stepping back and roaming his gaze over me. He smirks and I roll my eyes as he holds out his hand. I accept it and he leads me into the kitchen.

There are several young men standing around a counter filled with alcohol. Young women stand next to each of them, and everyone is in costumes.

"I think you've seen Grace, Kelsie, and Lucy around campus with me before." He sweeps an arm out to encompass the three smiling beauties in the living room. "And these are their boyfriends and my former teammates, Emmett, Killian, and Hayes."

I smile and wave. "Nice to officially meet you all." There's a round of "nice to meet you's" and handshakes.

The tall blonde, who I think is Kelsie, chimes in. "We need to open up a bottle of something to toast the extraordinary woman who finally brought our Hendy here down to his knees."

"Here, here!" the big guy named Killer says.

"Hey, Lottie. We just opened this bottle of wine my dad sent. He's in Tuscany with his new girlfriend," Grace says with a cheerful smile, pouring the dark red liquid into a Red Solo cup. Ahh. Reminds me of my uni days. "Would you like some?"

"Thanks. I love Tuscany." I sniff the fragrant wine and then take a sip, immediately noting the varietal components. "Mmm...a Brunello di Montalcino."

Killian looks at Joel. "Whoa, bro. Your professor knows her wines."

Joel gives him a good punch on the arm. "Dude, she's NOT my professor anymore."

I feel the heat wash over my cheeks and take another fortifying drink.

"Sorry." Killian apologies with a frown.

Grace rolls her eyes and Kelsie laughs. "Don't mind Killer...he's always been this dumb."

We all chuckle but Grace sticks up for her boyfriend, wrapping her arms around his tree trunk-sized neck. I don't know what they feed this chap, but he's a mighty big one.

"Come on, baby. We don't have to take that from her," she says in a soothing voice, throwing her friend a stink-eye glare, emphasized with a small raspberry noise. "Let's go upstairs and I'll remind you how smart you are."

Their departure is followed by *oohs* and *ahhs*, and a "Go get 'er, Killer."

Kelsie and Mac sit down at the large bench-style kitchen table and Joel and I take a seat across from them.

"So, Hayes, Joel tells me you're still playing for the team as the kicker?" I ask, hoping I got that right. I have to admit, even though Joel has shared a lot with me about the team and game, I honestly find it hard to understand American football.

He nods. "Yep. And even though we don't have our

former star QB, our season is off to a good start. Isn't that right, Coach?" Hayes grins at Joel.

"Yeah, you motherfuckers were sucking it until I showed up."

Kelsie snorts. "Oh, Hendy. I thought you were a changed man, but you're still full of yourself."

"What can I say?" he says with a smirk. "When you got it, flaunt it."

We finish the bottle of wine and Lucy and Emmett wander off from the kitchen, leaving just the four of us at the table.

"Hey, have you seen Journey around? I want to introduce her to Lottie," Joel says to Kelsie.

She looks at the time on her phone. "I think she should be home from her date soon. They went to the Pizza Station and then to a movie."

I was thrilled to learn that Joel had a younger sister attending CFU and found it sweet that he was so protective of her.

"I swear to God, if that hockey boy tries anything on my little sister, I will..."

I place a hand on his arm to calm him down. "Hey, why don't you give me that tour now?"

"Okay...let me show you around." He leans into my side and whispers in my ear, "And my bedroom."

I follow him through the lower level of the crowded house as he introduces me to a few other former teammates and friends before we make our way upstairs. With my hand in his, he takes us down a long hallway on the second floor and opens the door at the end of it.

"I have the primary suite," he explains, quickly shutting the door behind us, drowning out the sounds from the party below us. The only thing I can hear now is my heart thumping wildly in my chest.

I'm not sure what I expected Joel's room to be like but definitely not this. It's not your typical graduate student room. In it is a large four-poster mahogany bed with a dark blue comforter and matching sheets. He even has a fancy-looking throw pillow. There's a matching dresser, two night-stands, and an antique chair and ottoman in the corner. The room's color seems to perfectly match the sheets with a blue-on-blue striped pattern.

"Who helped you with your decor?" I ask, moving to the bureau to snoop around at his collection of photographs and trophies.

"My mom." He laughs and walks over to the chair, removing his white lab coat and sitting down. He still wears the blue scrubs and he most definitely looks the suave doctor part.

I press a hand to my chest. "Doctor, I don't feel well. I might need an exam."

With a wicked grin, he crooks a finger and beckons me to him. I move with a sexy sway of my hips, while his eyes remain glued to my body. I've never had a man stare at me this intensely.

I stop in front of him, our knees pressed together and he leans forward to run his hand along my bare thigh. I shiver from his light touch as his hand stops just at the hem of the short dress.

"Show me where it hurts and I'll make it all better." His voice is deep and gravelly, and I nearly collapse in on top of him when he cups me between my legs.

He slowly traces the creases at the top of my thigh with his finger and then skims beneath the silky fabric of my knickers. Thank God the music is loud downstairs, because the moan he elicits from my throat when he separates my folds and circles my clit is loud and needy.

My desire for him is so strong, I can barely remain standing.

"You're so wet for me," he murmurs, bending at his hips and kissing a trail along the inside of one leg before moving to the other. My hand grips at his shoulders as he slides his finger inside and thrusts in and out.

"That feels so good. I need more."

He moves his head away and removes his finger, a disgruntled growl of protest escaping my lips.

"Come here," he says, hands grasping my hips to pull me onto his lap. My knees squeeze into the tight space between his legs and the arms of the chair, locking me in place over his hard erection that tents his hospital scrubs.

We both breathe a sigh of relief, our chests heaving as he places a hand on the back of my head. Our lips crash together and I'm consumed by this man. I begin grinding shamelessly against him, needing to find my release.

"That's right, baby. Use me to get yourself off," he commands against my lips. His suggestive summons has me rocking back and forth, grinding and moving against him. He reaches between our bodies, stroking my clit with his thumb and coaxing me to come.

That's all it takes for me to go crashing into bliss. He captures my cries of ecstasy with his lips and the pleasure from the release begins to subside and I slowly return to reality.

When I open my eyes, he's watching me like I'm the most fascinating thing he's ever seen.

"What?" I cock my head to the side, noting the slickness between my legs.

"You're gorgeous," he says, leaning back in the chair. He

looks every part the former quarterback with his straining biceps and strong shoulders.

"You're not so bad yourself," I tease lightly, then wiggle to move off his lap but his hands stay firm on my hips.

"You're not going anywhere, Nurse. I need to give you that shot of medicine." His lips cover mine in a demanding kiss when suddenly there's a loud commotion in the hallway.

"Hendy! Where the fuck are you, bro? Team shots!" Killian's voice calls out, then hard-knocks on the door.

He groans and I fight a giggle, but he presses a finger to my lips with a slow shake of his head. "Shh...don't say a word."

"Don't be a cockblocker, Killer! I'm kinda busy in here," he says and from the other side of the door, Killer yells, "Getting laid!"

"Go the fuck away."

Inspiration hits me then and I scoot off Joel's lap and land on my knees in front of him. His eyes go from irritated at Killer to downright dark as midnight when he realizes what I'm about to do.

"Are you trying to seduce me, Professor?"

I loosen the knot at the front of his scrubs and untie the strings. The material opens and I slide it down to expose his erection that springs free, and I grasp it firmly in my hand.

"You're not my student anymore. So, yes, I am trying to seduce you." I give him a short, hard stroke, and he groans. "In fact, sucking you off has been my fantasy for weeks. Now be quiet and let me do it." Then I wrap my lips around the head of his cock and eagerly swallow him down.

"Oh fuck, Lottie. You're killing me."

It doesn't take much to get him to the point of no return and within minutes, the muscles of his thighs tighten underneath my hands and his curses grow louder, and he is soon releasing his hot orgasm down my throat.

As we clean ourselves up in his bathroom, I stare at our reflections in the mirror and wonder how I'll feel going back downstairs to the party, to a room full of college-aged students.

I pause for a second and consider whether I'm even bothered by it. None of the students I met are my students. And even if they were, I don't think I'd care. I'm with Joel now and everyone knows it.

He's no longer a student of mine. He's not a quarterback anymore. He's a coach. And he's also my boyfriend.

Holy shit, he's my boyfriend.

"What?" Hendy asks, his reflection looking back at me with a concerned expression. "Everything okay?"

"Yes, it's nothing," I murmur as heat creeps up my cheeks. He gives me a pointed look and I shrug, searching his eyes. "I was just looking at you and thinking how hot my boyfriend is."

He's perfectly still for a long moment and then a grin spreads across his gorgeous face. "Well, I think my girlfriend is pretty fucking hot too," he says, leading me back out to the hallway with a possessive grip on my butt.

"Is that so?"

"Of course. Arguably, every quarterback in the history of football ends up with the hottest women," he says matter-of-factly.

I roll my eyes and press my forehead to his. "Yeah, but you aren't a quarterback anymore."

"I'm one better...I'm a quarterback coach who just scored himself a fucking A+ professor."

And just like that, we're a couple.

Despite all that we went through to get here, I'm truly

happy for the first time in a very long time. And as we re-enter the party and I listen to him and his former teammates tell stories, I realize I've fallen hard for this former quarterback.

Maybe I even fell for him that first night all those months ago.

The End

About the Authors

USA Today & International Bestselling romance author, **S.E. Rose** lives near Washington D.C. with her family.

When she's not wrangling her cats or keeping up with her kids, she's plotting her next story.

She loves all things wine, coffee, and cats.

In her non-existent free time, she enjoys traveling, going to concerts, binging on her favorite shows, and reading, especially if it's a good mystery or comedy.

Learn more about upcoming books from S.E. Rose at www.seroseauthor.com or follow her on Facebook and Instagram.

Sierra Hill is a ***RONE Award-Winning*** author of ***Game Changer***, as well as over 40 novels, including the college sports series, ***Courting Love***, and her newest hockey series, ***Vancouver Vikings***.

Subscribe to her email list and download a FREE book here: https://www.sierrahillbooks.com//newsletter

Read all the CFU crew series and More

College football - CFU Series

Falling for the Fake Boyfriend (Lucy and Emmett)

Falling for the Roommate (Grace and Killian)

Falling for the Football Player (Kelsie and Hayes)

Falling for the Quarterback (Hendy and Lottie)

Looking for some steamy small Town/firefighter/Brothers action?

Check out our co-written Fanning the Flames series

Burned

Ignited

Scorched

www.ingramcontent.com/pod-product-compliance
Lightning Source LLC
Chambersburg PA
CBHW030148010826

48973CB00002B/774